My Friend Natalia

My Friend Natalia

A NOVEL

LAURA LINDSTEDT

Translated from the Finnish by David Hackston

LIVERIGHT PUBLISHING CORPORATION
A Division of W. W. Norton & Company
Independent Publishers Since 1923

Copyright © 2019 by Laura Lindstedt
Original edition published by Teos Publishers, Finland, as *Ystäväni Natalia*
The English-language edition published by agreement with Laura Lindstedt and Elina Ahlback Literary Agency, Helsinki, Finland

Translation copyright © 2021 by W. W. Norton & Company, Inc.

Illustrations on pp. 41 and 205 © Jarkko Mikkonen

Niki de Saint Phalle, words from "My Men" © 2020 Niki Charitable Art Foundation. All rights reserved / ARS, NY / ADAGP, Paris

Lines of poetry by Freyja Kulkunen, credit: Katariina Vuorinen

All rights reserved
Printed in the United States of America

For information about permission to reproduce selections from this book, write to Permissions, Liveright Publishing Corporation, a division of W. W. Norton & Company, Inc., 500 Fifth Avenue, New York, NY 10110

For information about special discounts for bulk purchases, please contact W. W. Norton Special Sales at specialsales@wwnorton.com or 800-233-4830

Manufacturing by Lake Book Manufacturing
Production manager: Lauren Abbate

Library of Congress Cataloging-in-Publication Data

Names: Lindstedt, Laura, 1976– author. | Hackston, David, translator.
Title: My friend Natalia : a novel / Laura Lindstedt ; translated from the Finnish by David Hackston.
Other titles: Ystäväni Natalia. English
Description: New York : Liveright Publishing Corporation, [2021] | Includes bibliographical references.
Identifiers: LCCN 2020043557 | ISBN 9781631498176 (hardcover) | ISBN 9781631498183 (epub)
Classification: LCC PH356.L55 Y7813 2021 | DDC 894/.54134—dc23
LC record available at https://lccn.loc.gov/2020043557

Liveright Publishing Corporation, 500 Fifth Avenue, New York, N.Y. 10110
www.wwnorton.com

W. W. Norton & Company Ltd., 15 Carlisle Street, London W1D 3BS

1 2 3 4 5 6 7 8 9 0

My Friend Natalia

I am a psychologist, and I shouldn't discuss my clients' affairs. But on this occasion I will make an exception, as my former client—let's call her "Natalia"—encouraged me to share her story. Her case might offer comfort to those women, and why not men too, struggling with similar problems. "Natalia" herself came up with this suggestion during one of our sittings.

Well, no, let's correct that right away, so there's no misunderstanding: she did not sit. My habit of referring to these sessions as "sittings" dates back to a time when I still believed in solution-focused therapy. Back then, my clients and I would sit opposite each other in soft, comfortable armchairs, my own a shade of almond green, the client's Russian blue. We sank against the backrests or, if the situation required it, we leaned closer toward each other; connected by our body language, we vigorously worked through a problem, be it of the classification F10-19.1, F43.2 or F50.2.

"Natalia" was one of my first clients to lie on her back without prompting. When I showed her round my office, which I had rented in an apartment next to my house, I told her about the *couch*. It was on that *couch* that "Natalia" would lie down if she chose me as her therapist, if she decided that of all the psychotherapists in this city, I was the one best suited to help her. Qualifications were very important to "Natalia." She didn't want to talk to any old shrink; she wanted a highly specialized professional.

I was immediately enchanted by the way in which "Natalia" walked into my office. At our initial meeting, the client generally sits in the armchair, the Russian blue one, and allows their eyes to roam the space. They are cautious and confused, glancing surreptitiously at the *couch*, which I show them and where, if all goes well, they will lie down next time and the process will begin. The *couch* has no backrest or armrests, but I still call it a *couch*, because referring to it as a bed would irrevocably break something within my clients. And so, in their minds, they examine that *couch*, upholstered in terra-cotta orange, and they register the painting hanging above it. A few of them even correctly identify the artist, and at such moments a flicker of joy flares within me (one that I nonetheless quickly suppress for reasons of professional ethics): how wonderful that I might soon begin working with a fellow art lover.

But "Natalia" did not sit in the Russian blue armchair, which I offered her just as I offer it to every potential client. I don't force them, but I gesture toward the chair, slightly opening my hand as I do so. I nod in encouragement, subtly, after which I leave them in peace for a moment. I turn my back for a few seconds to pick up my notepad from the small table next to the almond-green armchair, an armchair that, like the Russian blue one, I had transferred over from my former office at the Merikenno Therapy House.

But as I have mentioned, "Natalia" did not sit in the armchair. She stepped into the room with a notable brashness and stood right on the stylized, four-leaf medallion pattern in the middle of the Persian rug on the floor.

When they first step into my office, my potential clients often appear shrunken, smaller than their real size. They don't know where to put their hands when they sit down, in their lap or on the armrests. They wait for me to steer the situation, to move things forward, which after all is my job and something I do gladly. But "Natalia" was not shy, rather her first words were: "Until the mid-nineties, that painting above the bed was in my grandmother's living room!"

"Natalia" took a step off the flower medallion on the rug and toward the painting, examining it as if through fresh eyes, turning her head to one side, as though she were trying to suck the gaudy colors into her reservoir of memories, a place we would spend the following months exploring and examining in detail. Then she let out a small, involuntary moan, a sound with a hint of both sorrow and pleasure, of that I am sure.

From that moment on, we began building mutual trust, a trust markedly different from that which exists between me and my other clients.

Natalia—from whose name I will now remove the quotation marks as I might remove the safety catch from a gun—had a problem that greatly impacted her everyday life. It might not have affected her so much, or grown to such proportions, if she had had a normal safety net around her—family, for instance, or a close circle of friends, the kind of friends you can tell about life's joys and sorrows so that the former grow and boom like the spring ice while the latter shrink to the wisps of a dandelion clock that mere words can puff into motion. When put into words, these achenes unravel and float away from the magic of a circle of friends—if a person has friends—only to land somewhere else, for the amount of sorrow in the world doesn't diminish when we talk about it, it simply takes seed elsewhere for a while. But if you talk a lot, the sorrow might permanently change shape. When sorrow is, as it were, made flesh right there on my couch—from which, like removing a bedspread, I will now remove the italics, that invention of the Florentine-Venetian Renaissance—when, lying on their back and letting go, there in the safe, snowy dugout of trust, the client puts their grief into words, that grief can change and turn into an unrecognizable, lace-edged nostalgia. If I didn't believe in this basic principle, I would have to change profession.

Natalia was still standing on the rug. She found it easier to speak standing up, or so she said, as though her upright frame gave this initial presentation of her problem more power. She pulled back her shoulders, positioned the supporting muscles in her upper body and walked in a small, relaxing circle. "I'm ashamed," she said with a nervous chuckle. "I'm so ashamed that I think I could faint!" She certainly didn't look faint. She looked as though she was preparing for a triple jump.

And so Natalia began to tell me what was bothering her. Her lovers were the most vexatious of her problems, just as they were the very salt of her life, the sugar, the marzipan, the umami. "They are gone, but they are still in my head," she said. "They are gone in the most profound sense, though they are with me— inside me, even! The more I kiss them, the less they are there. And then they are gone again. They walk out the door, they go to work, to their homes, their wives, their dogs. My brain starts to conjure up all kinds of situations in which I place them. Of course, I place myself in these situations too. I am always there, right in the center, and they press inside me through all possible orifices, and I feel myself filling up, but it never ends, and my head starts to ache. And there's no room inside me for a single sensible, progressive thought because my head is full of all these lovers—who are now gone. There's no room in me for information. I can't learn anything, I just become stupider by the day because my lovers are plowing away inside me. And soon I will lose my mind. I carry out my own work with all the lanterns extinguished, as it were, and soon the day will come when my boss will notice everything."

I interrupted her to ask what she did for a living. She told me she was one of a team of five graphic designers at a midsized PR company. Her job was to visually enhance the client's core message, and she loved her work. She wanted to develop herself, both professionally and—primarily—in her private life, to improve herself, but her imagination and her firmly held resolutions were galloping in opposite directions. That was why she had come to me.

"I imagine my boss creeping up behind me and noticing that my mouse hand isn't touching the mouse at all. He doesn't grab me and shake me awake in that boss-like manner of his, and he certainly doesn't thrust his hands beneath my arms to lift me onto the desk and lay me down on my stomach. The whole idea is impossible, senseless—after all, we're in an open-plan office. My boss has never abused his position of power. He doesn't tug my skirt up or pull down my tights and panties, after which he doesn't drop his pants to his ankles. This series of movements is far too complicated, now that I'm trying to explain it. But let's assume for a moment that we are naked from the waist down, my boss and I, me with my stomach on the desk and he behind me. The office around us is darkened, the phones have stopped ringing and the other employees have disappeared. My boss stands behind me, his large, hard member against my open, moist pudenda, and then: nothing. I repeat: nothing! In my mind I darken the office further still, like a magician I make the people disappear, the sounds of work stop, until there is only this strange, heavy breathing behind me. Let's add that too. You understand?

"I think about sex all the time. That is my problem. The act forces its way into my mind like a tumor, and I am lost. I've contemplated chemical castration, anti-androgens, I've even considered suicide. I know *in theory* what constitutes a healthy sex life, what a healthy relationship is like, but I am able to use those insights about as well as I can play the piano. That's right, I haven't got an ear for music. I experience everything—literally everything—as images. And I don't know what to do with my lovers who are absent when they are present and present when they are absent, and that's why I've come here, you're my last hope. Help me."

Thus spoke Natalia, and having uttered the final word of her monologue, she started to cry.

Something flared within me, and it wasn't merely sympathy, the emotion I feel for most of my clients. It was more like a sudden experience of harmony, wholly inappropriate given the circumstances. That seismic tremor placed what Natalia had just said in a frame, and not just any frame but something more akin to a Florentine tabernacle, a 24-carat gold-leaf glow, so powerfully did I experience her woes. Indeed, why beat around the bush: when Natalia started to cry, I had a potent sense that I was in the presence of beauty.

It wasn't the weeping Natalia who caused this impression. She wasn't particularly photogenic when she was crying. I wouldn't necessarily call her beautiful either, at least not in the traditional sense of the word. The distance between her mouth and eyes was greater than scientifically proven patterns of beauty would allow, and the distance between her eyes contravened the rules of symmetry too, because they were too close together, though she skillfully obscured the fact with makeup.

Right away I knew that here I had the kind of client I'd been waiting for all my life. This suffering individual might benefit from a method I developed in association with my mentor and which I fervently defended in my PhD, which received a grade of *cum laude approbator*, no less. Still, after my graduation the Finnish Association of Psychoanalysis did not accept me as a member, a matter that my mentor thought scandalous. He is currently collecting signatures from the more progressive members of our field in a petition demanding that my application be reassessed.

I felt the urge to take Natalia in my arms, though naturally I didn't do this. I suppressed my zeal and spoke in tones as dulcet as I could: "Thank you, Natalia, thank you for telling me so keenly about your problems." Then I said to her: "I wrote my PhD on methods that might be of use to you. I see you have a very vivid imagination, lots of cultural capital and the courage to speak out."

To make sure it didn't sound as though I was working on commission, like a door-to-door salesman thrusting products at unsuspecting customers, I told her about other available options. For clients, especially female clients, it's important to create the impression that they can choose, they can pick the red ball or the blue ball, though both fly just as far. Having said that, the choice between my method and standard methods is not a choice between a red or blue ball, it's more like the choice between a pétanque boule and a superball: you see, my method is designed to bounce and rebound.

I told Natalia that we could of course undertake a more traditional "in-and-out" therapy style, one that I offer most of my clients for the simple reason that they rarely have the time or indeed the gumption for the kind of preparations involved in the exercises I offered Natalia.

We agreed on a date for our next appointment, for which I promised to prepare a more detailed presentation of my method, and for which, exceptionally, I decided not to charge her. Not that I thought Natalia was living on the breadline, but because I wanted to create as stress-free an environment as possible, and money always creates tensions no matter how much we try not to think about it, even in circumstances where, to coin a phrase, money is meaningless. And yet, even when money is allegedly meaningless, it still means everything: tables, coats, dogs, watches, rings, cars, addresses, everything. A minuscule amount of money has meaning too, even if you give it to a beggar; a single minted coin has meaning, otherwise we wouldn't give it away, this miserable penny whose sheen wore off years ago, a measly shilling, its insides made of layered metal, nickel silver, circles of copper and nickel, but not a grain of gold, not even silver—even a lowly coin like this carries meaning and will carry that meaning until the end of days.

When Natalia arrived at my office the following week, I suggested that she sit in the Russian blue armchair. As I have said, the preliminary assessment before the start of treatment is conducted in that armchair. But again the chair didn't take her fancy. She preferred the couch. She didn't want to rest her legs, tired from walking here, at a ninety-degree angle—which sitting in the armchair apparently forces upon anyone sitting there, though next to the chair stands a navy blue footstool excellent for putting one's feet up, and which Natalia must surely have noticed; she noticed everything.

I must admit that I did recoil slightly at this, though again I concealed my emotions, and Natalia sat down on the couch, sideways to me, her back against the wall. Her unkempt, flaxen hair touched the bottom edge of the painting, and her feet stuck out in front of me like a couple of rolled-up antique maps.

"So tell me," she simpered. "What have you got up your sleeve to spin my head?"

Not a trace of the uncertainty, the tears, the angst. Was this the same woman who only a week ago awoke within me an unwavering desire to help?

I set to work, began introducing her to the program of exercises that, if she followed them, would undoubtedly help improve her sex life. Natalia in turn asked me a series of questions, three of which I had guessed in advance:

"What if, when I arrive at our sessions, I find I want to talk about something altogether different from what I've prepared for the exercises?"

"What if I can't come up with anything, should I turn up empty-handed?"

"What if my skills aren't up to this?"

"Will you be angry if I am bad at this?"

I tried to reassure her. It doesn't matter, we'll improvise together. You can always come to our sessions, even empty-handed. And I won't get angry, Natalia, it's impossible to make me angry.

"And these types of exercises, which you're suggesting I undertake, is there really scientific proof of their efficacy?" she asked, almost goading me, as if to insinuate that I might have obtained my doctoral degree from some faculty of pseudoscience or a mail-order university that I'd paid in hard cash. But I am used to living among people who like to question the validity of everything, and I had carefully prepared myself for this type of provocation.

I told Natalia that I had successfully deployed the layering method before, albeit to combat problems of a rather different caliber. I didn't see any reason why Natalia's feeling of malaise couldn't be alleviated using these exercises. "In these therapy sessions we will not primarily be looking to trace your memories," I told her. "Memories will resurface, that is clear, and they are most welcome. Nothing is off-limits. But in this process memories are only the raw material, we can't fully trust their veracity, they don't necessarily prove anything. You will write, you will allow your hand to guide your thoughts like a conductor leading an orchestra with a baton. You will give your mind a form. Even bullet points are fine, you can use them to start developing your ideas. We will uncover different strata of memories and layer them up again. And this we will continue as long and as diligently as necessary, until whatever it is that's gnawing away at you, whatever is hurting you, loses its power and eventually turns into something else. Black will become red, red will become green, green violet, violet yellow, and so on. We're going to create new mental paths in your mind. We'll fill the old, deeply ingrained tracks with fresh, fertile soil. And from that soil your brave new life will flourish, Natalia. In my company we can safely reap the harvest of that work."

Natalia listened to my introduction with her eyes closed. She was either fully concentrated or entirely lost in thought.

I only had to wait a few seconds before she gave a smile, nodded, opened her eyes and turned to face me. "I am prepared to commit myself to the program. This could be fun!"

Doubt flickered through me. It would be dishonest not to put that on the record. Did she simply accept what I had offered just like that? *Black will become red, red will become green, green violet, violet yellow* . . . What on earth was I thinking when I said that? Why hadn't she burst out laughing at that point, specifically at that point? Was she really this easily led?

I was jumping to conclusions, and I knew it immediately. Natalia had come to me looking for help. The fact that she hadn't sat down in the armchair I'd indicated but decided instead, almost shamelessly, to assume her own space in the small office didn't mean that she would argue over every point or try to laugh me out of the room. As eccentric as she was, based on our two initial meetings, she was primarily (this is how I instantly rebuked myself, though perhaps not in these exact words) *a woman in need.* All the words I threw in her direction would tug her further away from that oppressive obsession that made her cry whenever she tried to talk about it. The color metaphors that spilled from my mouth, *black will become red, red will become green,* and so on, were merely words among other words, no better or worse than other words. Why would Natalia waste her time with me if she didn't genuinely trust my professionalism?

I suggested we start with a simple pain-displacement exercise, and she seemed instantly enthused at the idea. I gave her a few books from my shelf as inspiration but stressed that she didn't have to read them, she didn't even need to open them, and she must under no circumstances feel under any pressure regarding them; if the books began to cause her distress, she could decide not to open the bag I put them in, she could put the bag at the back of her closet, if she had one, and forget all about them because I didn't need those books anymore.

"But they might be of some use," I said as I showed her to the door. "If you feel helpless, if you feel that you don't know what to do or where to start, then pick up a book. You might find something interesting just by flicking through, a simile that suddenly hits the layers of pain right out of the park. This petrified pain will start to crumble, and words will start to bubble out of you. By looking behind the images that cause you pain, under my guidance you will learn your very own language, Natalia, the words to wrap around your obsessions. In a year's time you'll wonder who on earth you were, whose desires you really desired."

RECOVERY PROGRAM
WEEK 1

Pain-displacement exercise.
Instruction: Think of a situation that has hurt you.
Rewrite the situation using new words.
If necessary, borrow other people's words.

Natalia's first official session was every bit as memorable as our first encounter. From her bag she took out an enormous chrome-plated alarm clock, an old-fashioned mechanical one with large, bold numbers on the dial, and which makes an almighty racket when triggered by the timer mechanism. Then she lay down on the couch, pulled up her knees and placed the clock on her stomach.

I will admit the alarm clock disturbed me. It was a provocation. Keeping an eye on the passing of time is my job. My clients should be able to trust that, almost without their noticing, I will steer their words toward the point where I gently say, "Well, that seems to be all we have time for today."

Apparently this wasn't good enough for Natalia. She wanted to steer her words herself and to fall silent at a time of her own choosing. From our very first session, she stopped talking a few minutes before the hour was up. Those final moments we spent in silence. The clock ticked loudly and together we listened as the seconds passed, seconds that only a moment ago had been buried beneath our voices but which were now impossible not to notice. I always ended our sessions at the agreed time, to do otherwise would have been out of the question, but Natalia wanted this silence, so naturally I conceded.

Natalia had prepared for our first session by writing a little vignette, which by mutual agreement we called a pain-displacement exercise, just as a certain type of dog is called a guide dog or a certain color of horse is called a bay. Natalia pulled a piece of paper from inside her bra, which, in light of what was to happen next—if I may preempt by setting the reader's horizon of expectation appropriately—was just a gentle warm-up.

She opened the sheet of paper, which she had folded into four, and began to read: "Tonight . . ." Then she clasped the paper to her breast and murmured something.

"Could you repeat that? I couldn't quite make that out," I asked, and Natalia sighed.

She composed herself again, rebuilding the strength that this single word, *tonight*, had seemingly erased from her. I found this curious. After all, so much romantic tosh began with that word.

"I'm nervous. You understand?" she said. "I didn't conjure this little story off the top of my head. As a starting point I used a poem I found in one of the books you gave me and changed some of the words. Well, quite a lot of them, actually. In fact, there might not be any of the original words left, not in the same order at least, but the feel of the poem is still there. I'm sure you'll guess straightaway which text I mean! I've also deconstructed the original and reorganized the words. The silences of the original poem didn't work here at all, they didn't help express what *I* wanted to express"—Natalia almost spat the pronoun from her mouth—"and they made me feel somehow fake, artificial. But the original poem is there all the same. It inspired me, encouraged me, and I even came up with a new name for the text, which is . . . *ta-daa! . . . In the Courtyard at the Ukrainian Embassy!* Please don't ask why that's the title. Okay. Here we go."

Tonight I plan to really let myself go. To lose control so that every-thing goes to hell. So that the gray men of authority turn up, the reflective strips on their pants legs glinting. I lie on the darkened ground, open my mouth wide and shout into the dirt. A gray man of authority places his boot against my head and presses it down. I smell the moist earth. The grass is dead, yellowed. I lift myself up, thrash and struggle until I buckle in two, and when I double over like a pocketknife I stop putting up a fight. I slump, a resilient piece of chewing gum stuck in my hair. A thin mattress against the con-crete floor. Did I already mention that urine smells? Did I already mention that I am a victim of violence? Did I already mention that I am a victim of institutionalized violence—an innocent victim, no less? Did I already mention that the patriarchy rapes me? That I love you? Push, oh my love, my darling, shove your knuckleduster-clad fist into my pussy.

To my embarrassment I didn't recognize the source text. There were various reasons for this, the most likely of which was the fact that most of the poetry collections I owned, which now belonged to Natalia, I had received as a gift from a former client who was a poet. The man had only published one volume of original poetry, entitled *Donkey Milk*, and even that was decades ago. He had sought out therapy in order to overcome a bout of writer's block; he always brought me the newest anthologies and wanted me to read them so we could discuss poetry together, and I read them because that's what he was paying me for. The client lived in a very expensive neighborhood, he had plenty of old money to his name. He dabbled in the stock market all day long so that he didn't have to think about poetry, much less about writing it, and that's why he came to me. And so for forty-five minutes every week he thought about poetry here in my office and forced me to do the same, though unfortunately this didn't resolve his writer's block. Over time he began speculating on the market more and more, and eventually, not a moment too soon, he stopped coming to see me. The books remained here in my office, but the memory of reading them faded the minute our professional relationship ended—and it was a good thing it did.

Natalia waited for my comments, almost holding her breath, and I began. I described the end of her text as "surprising" and asked to see the paper for a moment so I could think of some follow-up questions.

To respect Natalia's wishes, we spoke about everything except the title of the poem. I asked, for instance, what she meant by "the gray men of authority" and whether they represented "the patriarchy" that had "raped" her and, indeed, what "rape" meant in this context. I also asked whether she had ever actually been raped. This she denied. I asked whether she had been arrested or restrained, but she had no firsthand experience of this either.

"But you have been in love?" I asked, and Natalia gave a quiet moan, which I took as a yes.

All of a sudden Natalia began describing a situation in which she had found herself, partly by accident and partly through her own fault, which had traumatized her greatly and which the text she had compiled metaphorically represented, or so she claimed. Once she started, she carried on talking until, without warning, she stopped and asked, as if she had just woken from a dream: "Has my pain been displaced now? And what should I do with this piece of paper?"

I was thrilled: my method appeared to be working with Natalia. Barely able to conceal my satisfaction, I asked what she wanted to do with the paper. She said she wanted to leave it with me for the time being, and I agreed to keep it safe. I asked what she felt now.

"Empty," she replied. And her answer was as empty as the emptiest of empty buckets, like a wineglass nobody had ever filled, her voice imparted nothing, it was colorless, monotone, and I could see that misery had begun to push its way into her mind.

But as Natalia spoke, I had noted down some key words regarding her traumatic experience. I tore the page from my notepad, handed it to her and said: "Let's continue with this exercise! Here are some new words you can use. These are your own words, the words you have just used, but I suggest you now do something quite different with them. Now you will harness them to serve another kind of memory. I suggest the following: Seeing as your poem, or rather the poem from which you constructed your own metaphorical story, brought up the subject of 'men,' 'rape' and what you referred to as 'pussy' and the act of 'shoving' into that 'pussy,' in the next exercise you might start exploring these challenging subjects using the supporting words I've collated here. In that way we can continue discussing your sexuality *per se*—that's why you're here, after all. How does that sound?"

Natalia was quiet, and for a moment I was worried. Had I moved too quickly? Did she understand what I was suggesting? I hadn't noticed that Natalia was staring at the clock, that she had noticed the minute hand anxiously pushing toward the end of our session, and that she had already brought our session to a close by closing her mouth. To her it didn't matter that my question was left hanging, unanswered.

The alarm clock started rattling. Natalia remained silent. She left it to trill, allowing it, as it were, to speak for itself, to shout and curse and rage in an earsplitting, metallic racket. That's how I interpreted her decision not to switch it off, and that's how I coped with the noise, though I was inclined to throw the thing out the window.

Eventually Natalia switched off the alarm, stood up from the couch and opened her mouth. "Our time is up. I like your suggestion. It inspires me. I already know what I'm going to work on using these words. I'm going to write about pornography. In fact, this all relates rather viscerally to my childhood. It's quite possible that many of my life's contortions stem from that time . . ."

I got up from my almond-green chair to shake her hand, as I do with all my clients at the end of a session—all except one woman who suffered from chirophobia and lived in mortal fear of other people's hands. I was trying to overcome my surprise that Natalia had said *our time is up*, that she had used my words, words that so far I hadn't had the opportunity to use in her presence. And it was my own fault. The alarm clock had fazed me.

I gripped Natalia's hand more firmly than I'd intended. I squeezed so hard that she pulled away and looked up at me, perplexed. I smiled and decided that I wouldn't allow this to happen again. When the alarm clock rang at the end of next week's session, I would take immediate control of the situation. I would say and, if necessary, holler above the noise, *Well, it seems our time is up*, and Natalia would switch off the clock and we could bid each other goodbye in an orderly, professional manner.

I took a step toward the hallway, which Natalia had already reached. I tried to think beautiful thoughts about her alarm clock. I tried to see it as a friend, a colleague, someone I was collaborating with toward a common goal, that goal being, of course, Natalia's improvement, the illuminating flame that with my help would flicker into life and burn her illness to ashes. In fact, it was at that moment that I realized I would simply have to deal with the presence of the alarm clock, that it was something truly nonnegotiable.

RECOVERY PROGRAM
WEEK 2

Thoughts on pornography.
Instruction: Use the supporting words I wrote down.

"I'm sorry I canceled last week's session at the last minute, but my preparation was incomplete. I'll tell you why in a moment. Let me start a bit further back—and not with this week's official subject matter. I'd like to start with a thinker named Jean-Paul Sartre. You've heard of him, I assume? Wait a moment, I'll take out the piece of paper I've used to jot down my thoughts. That is, Sartre's thoughts, and not only his . . . I guess half of humanity must think like this. Perhaps you do, too?"

Thus began our second therapy session, to which Natalia arrived like a whirlwind, sweaty and out of breath because she had biked all the way to my office. She'd decided to take up cycling, or so she told me on the telephone a week ago when she rescheduled our appointment, because she found that thinking about our pornography exercise had left her with "shocking amounts of excess energy." She suddenly noticed that her alertness was "sky-high" and this "excess energy" prevented her from sleeping. She tried to calm herself with physical exercise, by going from one place to another by bike. She had no time for other, more focused types of exercise, as she was apparently "crazily serious" about our work together. And when she said this—let me remind you that we were speaking on the telephone—I had to control myself. I was about to tell her that unfortunately I'd have to bill her for the unused session in its entirety. This rule is clearly outlined on my website, and I tell every client about it at our first meeting: *If a therapy session is canceled for reasons other than a force majeure less than five days before the session in question, the client will be charged for the missed session in full.* The deferment that Natalia was asking for would leave an eighty-five-euro hole in my accounts, and she had the gall to call me only thirty minutes before we were due to meet.

So I was on the verge of bringing Natalia back to earth, of sitting her down face-to-face with the realities of life, when she said: "I need to tell you something terrible, my dear doctor. I stayed home from work today, I told them I had an unbearable migraine. But our exercise was still nowhere near ready! Besides, my head was about to explode. I felt dizzy and nauseous. I imagined I'd be able to get all this done in a single day, but it didn't happen that way. I'm crazily serious about my work with you, this is more important than anything else. Please forgive me."

I must admit, Natalia's dedication thrilled me, and on top of that I felt almost moved when she called me her "dear doctor." Of course, such an old-fashioned phrase seemed very out of place in the circumstances; I'm not a doctor but a researcher with a PhD in psychology. That being said, Natalia's words did not knock my powers of judgment off-kilter. I deliberately pushed aside the disappointment that this small financial inconvenience caused me and drew the relevant conclusions. Natalia's lack of preparedness, her near desperation, was a force majeure *par excellence*. Also, I was eager to see what she had been preparing so feverishly.

Natalia was deeply grateful. She promised hand on heart that she would never cancel an appointment at half an hour's notice ever again, and this promise she kept.

And now, there she lay in front of me, a sheet of notepaper in her hand, the alarm clock on her stomach, and challenged me with the words "Perhaps you do, too?"

"I found Sartre's idea in a feminist comic strip, which I got as a present from a friend in Sweden a few years ago. She's in women's studies, not *women's* studies, you see, though she is a woman— rather, she practices research in the field of women's studies. No, I mean . . . You don't *practice* research, do you, you practice weight lifting, horse riding. She *conducts* research for a living on a temporary contract. I gather they call it gender studies these days. But when I was still a student, it was women's studies.

"The book presented Sartre's unfathomable ideas in comic-strip format. It presented many other ludicrous patriarchal ideas too, but it was Sartre's idea that leapt to mind when I looked at the list of words you'd given me.

"Did I really use the word *hole* last time? I remember talking about there being 'a hole in my memory.' I spoke about how the conversation, which had occurred before a situation that had wounded me very gravely, had completely disappeared from my

mind. Did I talk about Shrove Tuesday buns, the constant debate
about whether they are better with jam or marzipan, did I swear
that marzipan is far superior? Did I speak about illegal settlements
or maybe the recently discovered dwarf planet far beyond the
Kuiper Belt? I don't know. At this point there is a hole in my
memory. And you wrote down the word 'hole.'

"Well, Sartre wrote a lot about holes.

"Sartre wrote: *The female organ is primarily a hole.*

"Sartre wrote: *The female organ is like all other holes, a plea for
existence.*

"Sartre wrote: *A woman pleads for foreign flesh, flesh that will fulfill
her by penetrating her, by splitting her asunder.*

"And he wrote: *A woman senses her role as a plea specifically because
she is 'hollow.'*

"That Swedish feminist comic strip ridicules Sartre's nonsense
very astutely. It made me laugh when I reread it last week. I almost
wet myself laughing! I thought of the ever-so-serious Simone de
Beauvoir, or rather the portrait of her on the cover of that magazine, the one where she's so serious, as though she's about to start
speaking, as though she's about to say, *I am Françoise, by the way,
Jean-Paul is Pierre, Olga K. is Xavière*—this was their complicated
triangle, you see, that Simone couldn't help but write about in
her first novel. But I know that Simone also knew how to laugh. I
did a Google image search and found lots of pictures of her smiling or laughing. In one of them she is aiming a gun at something
outside the photograph. Her eyes are closed, and there's a crooked
smile on her lips. Jean-Paul has his right hand on her shoulder;

he's smoking his pipe, terribly serious. Jean-Paul's eyes are open. I wondered whether Jean-Paul considered Simone a hole and a plea or whether it was only Olga K. and later Wanda and Bianca and what's-her-name that Jean-Paul considered a hole, a plea that he was only too happy to help fulfill. Did Jean-Paul consider Simone a woman at all? Or was she nothing but a pencil sharpener?

"At this point my thoughts regarding Sartre took a decidedly nasty turn. I thought of his eyes, darting here and there like a frog's—which was a rude thing to think, after all, because, unlike his thoughts, he couldn't do anything about his eyes. I thought of his little chin, his dirty, blackened teeth, and wondered how Simone— or anyone—could ever have kissed him. Maybe they never kissed?

"I think I already mentioned that they had what people nowadays call an 'open relationship.' What exactly did Sartre mean by such 'openness'? After a hard day's writing and thinking, did he eagerly fill all those gaping holes and pleas around him whenever Simone had other things to do, and did he use a condom—which by the way were freely available during the years of his Parisian promiscuity—or did he sow his seed directly into all those holes? I'm not entirely sure about the war years and the occupation. I mean, were condoms readily available back then? Still, I'm sure that, at that time, there were plenty of holes and pleas to go round, and not all of them were between women's legs.

"Once I had given enough thought to Sartre's ideas of holes and pleas, I began to approach this particular hole, plumbing my own thoughts and my own memories. Now we're getting to the important part—*ta-daa!*—the bit where I have scattered all your supporting words, casting them all around, without giving them too much thought. My notes are a mess . . . Goodness knows what's going to come of all this!"

Well—there seemed to be no limit to Natalia's mental gyrations! Of course, "we" weren't getting anywhere, though she claimed otherwise. Getting somewhere together would have required silence, pauses, my cautiously probing questions, her cautiously probing answers, but Natalia had prepared for our session like a star pupil. She couldn't help herself saying *ta-daa*, couldn't help beating her drum in time with the almost regal procession of her sentences. So certain she was of herself, of her arrival, her success.

I began to understand why she had needed an extra week. She wanted to twist me around her little finger.

I tried to sneak a look at what Natalia had written in her notepad, to see how comprehensively she had considered these thoughts, or someone else's thoughts, beforehand, though naturally the exercises I had prescribed didn't require such painstaking work. Did Natalia sense the shift in my posture? I didn't make the faintest sound, my clothes didn't rustle in the slightest, but somehow she suddenly started playing with the sheet of paper in her hand, waving it in front of her face like a fan.

"I was seven years old when I discovered a comic strip that wasn't remotely feminist in one of the paper recycling bins near our house. Of course, at home we didn't talk about feminism or any other isms, our home wasn't at all political, so I wouldn't have known a feminist comic if I'd tripped over one. Be that as it may, this one wasn't remotely feminist.

"The cartoon strip I dug up involved an adventure in the jungle. You could see that from the cover. It thrilled me because I'd always enjoyed Tarzan stories. On the cover of the cartoon strip there was a scantily clad, large-breasted woman with long, flowing hair. She was leaning against the lianas laughing, looking right at me.

"I remember that her bright white teeth looked even whiter than the feathers of the cockatoo sitting on the branch above her. It's only now as an adult, now that I've given the matter some thought, that I realize why that was. Her teeth were jewels, agates, pearls, they framed a great promise; and it was absolutely not a plea, it was a promise. Thank you for this supporting word, Doctor, 'promise' is precisely what I want to talk about right now.

"The promise was her mouth.

"Her mouth was transformative for me, because it worked in a way that as a seven-year-old I never could have imagined.

"I don't know what your childhood was like, Doctor, but in my childhood we all rummaged around in paper recycling bins because we thought we might find something forbidden, something that we had no business holding in our hands. And which, for that very reason, belonged to us. Adults kept close guard over their secrets, and that's why we needed secrets too. Besides, secrets weren't secrets if they were just agreements of confidentiality, if their betrayal wouldn't have destroyed anything. Secrets need to have a destructive power. Do you understand? And because children's living environments are geographically speaking very limited, we had to look for destructive secrets where we were most likely to find them—among things that have been thrown away, for example, perhaps even deliberately hidden from view.

"I quickly flicked through the A5-sized comic to see whether it might provide me with a secret. A tingling ran the length of my body when I realized just what kind of treasure I was holding.

"Naturally, I couldn't begin examining the comic there in the yard, but I saw *something*, and that *something* somehow heated me up. I wanted to flick through the comic immediately, from beginning to end, so that that *something* might flicker into view again only to disappear in a flash beneath the other pages, but I managed to control myself. I hid the comic beneath my shirt and tucked my shirt into my pants. I smuggled it into my room and stuffed it beneath my mattress.

"Once I was tucked up in bed, I silently pulled the magazine out again. I had a tiny little flashlight that was supposed to be a key ring, but I didn't keep my keys on it because I also had a teddy-bear key ring, and that was more important to me than the lamp. When I squeezed the bear in my fist—it was little and blue, sewn from a strip of denim fabric—I felt I was almost home, no matter where I was. The flashlight was cylindrical, clear-cut, and it fitted in my hand, but it was hard and cold whereas the teddy bear was soft and warm. Well, of course the bear wasn't actually warm. Fabric is rarely warm unless it's been in the sunshine, the clothes dryer or pressed against the radiator. But it was that softness that made the bear feel almost warm, the warmth was linked to its softness just as hardness is linked to cold. Above all I enjoyed the feel of the bear. I mean, I enjoyed the fact that the bear had a snout, ears, paws and a stumpy little tail, that the bear was multi-dimensional, unlike the lamp. When I squeezed it in my hand, the bear always felt radiant. It brought me inexplicable pleasure when I squeezed its extremities—particularly its snout—and it became all crumpled up, but not permanently. The lamp, meanwhile, remained cylindrical no matter what I did to it. Only striking it with my father's hammer would have made it multidimensional. But I didn't want to smash my lamp with a hammer; I'd received it as a birthday present from a girl I didn't particularly like but whom I always had to invite to parties because not inviting her would have upset her mother. And eventually I found a sensible use for the key-ring lamp. It lit the way on my nocturnal visits to the bathroom, which I had to make almost every night, often many times, only to realize that once I was sitting on the toilet I didn't need to wee at all. I was forbidden from shouting for help if the reason for waking up in the middle of the night was merely needing to go to the bathroom. My mother said I was old enough by now to shake myself out of the sense of fear caused simply by a full bladder. My mother thought it was a perfectly natural thing and didn't require any attention save for going to the toilet. I agreed with her in part and soon learned not to shout out.

"And so I switched on that tiny little lamp and started to read. I read both the images and the words, which were rather few and far between in the pages of the comic. I read diligently from start to finish, one page at a time, because I knew that the *something* was waiting for me at the end. And there was no reason to hurry toward the end, because hurry would only spoil the tingling.

"I don't have that comic anymore. In fact, I no longer have anything that has ever meant anything to me. I would have thrown it out myself sooner or later if my mother hadn't beaten me to it. I would have returned it to the recycling bin, hidden beneath my shirt. I still don't know how she found it. Perhaps the guilt was seeping out of me? Perhaps back then I was, as I am now, completely emotionally transparent?

"Nonetheless, I still remember fragments of the story surrounding that *something*. For instance, the fact that the white-toothed woman on the cover was fighting in the jungle. It might have had something to do with diamonds or buried treasure. It certainly had nothing to do with altruism or saving indigenous peoples. Of that I am sure. The woman was fighting in order to become rich, but in order to fight she needed enemies. And by that I mean real enemies, not an army of Hottentots whose warriors only stood as tall as the woman's nipples.

"I'm sorry, I know I should technically refer to them as the Khoekhoe people. I'm not an uncouth prick, you know. I won't speak like that anymore, ever, anywhere. Except here, that is, because I'm trying to channel the voice of my childhood.

"In the same breath, I must confess that conjuring up my memories has been very hard. Of course I know I'm allowed to present these stories any which way I want. We agreed on that. But if I'm honest, something about this is bothering me. All last week I tried to think of that *something*, firstly as myself, as the contemporary me. It wasn't hard, after all I've come across plenty of *somethings* throughout my adult life. And yet I was constantly unsatisfied, while at the same time I was utterly invigorated, until my state of mind suddenly became agitated. I was on the verge of collapse. I began drawing that *something* in order to control my nerves, to delve deeper and deeper. I really tried to remember. And I lost sleep over it. Then I called you and canceled our appointment. I drew and drew, destroyed and destroyed. I took inspiration first from pictures, then from a live model. Do you mind if we return to this drawing later?

"Perhaps I'm old-fashioned, but I wanted to relive the feeling that staring at that *something* caused me all those years ago— and not the feeling that thinking about that *something* awakes in me now.

"Let's try.

"No, sorry. *I'll try.*

"You can't help me, my dear doctor, not before you know everything about the hole around which this *something* is circling!

"In addition to the woman, there was a man in the comic strip too. He was perhaps less of a protagonist than the woman because his picture wasn't on the front cover but the back cover. The man was fighting in the jungle too. He fought for the same reasons as the woman, but they never fought on the same side because their goal was never a shared one. They were enemies. They both wanted to become rich. They didn't want to join forces and share the treasure, though this would have made their endeavors far easier and rendered the creation of the comic strip utterly pointless.

"Back then I understood—or rather my subconscious understood—that the man and the woman had to fight against one another so that the *something* could happen spontaneously, in other words, that it could happen for real and not just in a pretend, make-believe sense.

"Cat and mouse, the classic scenario. Once that scenario changed, when, say, one of them discovered a shortcut that wasn't marked on the map, the mouse became the cat and the cat the mouse. Cat and mouse, mouse and cat, each in turn, until there in the pallid light of the key-ring lamp I reached the centerfold, the only place where the silver staples showed through, tightly holding the sheets of paper together.

"There on the centerfold, the man and woman encountered one another.

"I could barely contain myself. I had conscientiously progressed from one page to the next, from one image to the next, but now my gaze did not so much as glance at the six rectangular frames on the left-hand page. Of course, I later returned to those six frames in an attempt to fully understand what the hell this so-called encounter was all about, but at this point all I could do was hurry onward. As if in a trance, I relinquished the rules of self-restraint that I had created for myself. You can't believe what shocking pleasure and tingling I felt by letting go!

"I squeezed both my legs tightly around my quilt, which by now had turned into a thick, twisted vine, because I wanted to imagine that I too was in the jungle. I stared at the image on the right-hand page, which featured only one large frame that wasn't really a frame at all because it didn't have a border. The page showed an image of the white-toothed, curly-haired woman's head, more specifically her profile, once, twice, three times, five times at least. The first head was right up against the top staples, the next slightly to the side and lower down. The woman's flowing hair was always hidden behind the previous head. Do you see what I mean?

"Let me explain.

"The lips of the uppermost head were slightly open, and the lips of each subsequent head were slightly more open until the woman's mouth was stretched wide. But unlike on the cover image, the woman never showed her teeth: now her gaping mouth was like that of an eel.

"At the third head, her eyes closed and remained closed until the end. That ending was at the lower right-hand edge of the page, toward which the woman's head was gently angled. Do you see? A bit like in Marcel Duchamp's *Nude Descending a Staircase*, which is itself a series of overlapping images. Duchamp's *Nude* is abstract, of course, while this image was entirely performative, and Duchamp's *Nude* is art, while this was just trash. But in this way the woman, or rather the woman's head, appeared to move inside the picture. Its many noses, eyes, lips and chins descended toward that *something* that I'd seen while flicking through the comic, that I now saw whole and from which I couldn't avert my eyes.

"Naturally I recognized that *something* as the male member. My father had one too, but it was nothing like this one. The veiny, erect member jutted up at the lower edge of the page, lonely and expectant. In light of my current knowledge, I might even say: it jutted upward as a plea! Surely something jutting upward can plead every bit as much as something opening inward. In a rather silly way, Sartre was wrong—yet again. I'm getting angry again . . . and amused. What the hell was that man really thinking when he opened his fly and pulled out his member, a member that was very likely more beautiful than his face? His erection didn't create philosophy or literature; it simply prayed to be enveloped by holes, pleaded for the soft, moist, slippery surface against its own, hardened skin.

"Sartre surely didn't think to himself: *My member is above all lonely and expectant.*

"Sartre didn't think this either: *My genitals are like all men's genitals: a plea for the waiting to end.*

"Sartre didn't think: *I plea for strange flesh so that it might change my being into something meaningful, by hiding me, sucking me dry, so that I may once again fill up.*

"And he most certainly did not think: *I sense my role as a plea for the simple reason that I will jut upward until I am spent.*

"But enough of Sartre! He was nothing but a terrible toad disguised as a philosopher.

"On the other hand, this comic strip through which, at the age of seven, I first encountered an erection, still makes me think today. Once I had been staring at that confusing page for a while, once I had stared at it and stared again at the right side of this page, tamed with silver staples, in which the woman's head was slowly lowering itself, mouth more and more open, toward that *something*, I did two things, in the following order. I turned the page, and in the very first frame something happened that even with my childlike understanding I'd guessed in advance: the woman's mouth concealed the man's member. His member disappeared. Only the woman's lips remained.

"After this I returned to the centerfold and read carefully through the six frames that in my excitement I had skipped over. Those frames told me a story. And I'm afraid that now that story was burned onto the scant mycelium of my mental capacity, singed into every cell, like porridge burnt to the bottom of a pot.

"I am embarrassed, but I will tell you.

"I'm sure you'll now draw a series of terrible conclusions about me when I tell you this, but I must remind myself—and you— that that is your job.

"The six-frame introduction to fellatio went as follows:

"Frame One: The man and woman, no longer the cat and the mouse, suddenly encounter each other in the jungle.

"Frame Two: From the folds of her loincloth, the woman pulls out a knife. The man raises his enormous hand into the air.

"Frame Three: The man and the woman dive at each other like leopards going in for the kill.

"Frame Four: The man and woman roll around on the ground. The knife flies off into the upper corner of the frame, the man having succeeded in wresting it from the woman's hand.

"Frame Five: The man tears open the woman's shirt, her enormous, fulsome breasts come into view. The woman's hand is in the man's pants.

"Frame Six: The woman has turned upside down and is grabbing at the man's crotch.

"The mouth opening—into which the jack-in-the-box that

sprung from inside the man's pants momentarily disappeared—changed forever the way I think of a woman's mouth. I could no longer look at my mother's mouth the same way. When my mother spoke, I imagined a veiny, black-and-white member coming out of nowhere and shutting her up. I couldn't even look at my own mouth in the mirror without imagining it full of such a member. This is strange, after all the woman in the comic voluntarily lowered the opening of her mouth to cover up the man's member, and the member didn't force its way into the woman's mouth but waited, patiently, at the bottom of the frame. A few frames later the woman lowered the hole between her legs to cover the man's member, but the sight of this no longer affected me, I don't know why.

"What I do remember is that the following day, while my mother was outside beating our rugs and my father was goodness-knows-where, I colored in the jungle woman's bright white teeth on the cover, turning them blue and red. I mean, every other tooth blue, every other tooth red."

Once Natalia had finished the story of the first significant hole in her life, she rolled onto her side and reached for the bag she had left beside the couch. (At our last meeting she had left the bag in the corridor outside.) She slid the sheet of paper inside the bag and pulled out another; this one too looked as though it was covered in writing. Then she pulled out a cardboard folder and from inside the folder she took a sheet of white paper and handed it to me.

I stared at the drawing. Natalia had sketched in pencil the image of a penis, more specifically an erection.

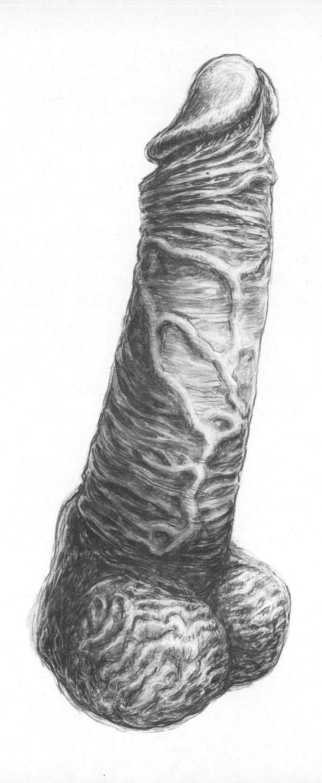

"This is a very accomplished work," I told her. "You have a gift with the pen."

The drawing immediately brought to mind Ebba Masalin's botanical teaching drawings, which I remembered admiring back in primary school, where they hung on the walls year after year. In front of me now I saw a knobbly, tasty tuber, something between a cabbage and a potato, I saw a zucchini, not the color but the shape.

In my estimation, at least, the erection that Natalia had drawn was substantial. I couldn't help thinking that only a moment ago Natalia had told me she took inspiration "first from pictures, then from a live model." It seemed she must have destroyed all the sketches she made from pictures; they hadn't satisfied her critical taste. Instead, the picture in my hands had been drawn from a live model. That's what her words must have meant: *first* means first, *then* means then.

And at that moment a shocking doubt washed over me. I realized Natalia's contention simply couldn't have been true. Drawing a picture like that doesn't happen all at once. At a modest estimate— if we assume, given the notable quality of the drawing, that Natalia is an experienced artist—it would take at least two hours to complete a work like this. The erection, on the other hand, could almost certainly not last that long, unless, that is, the model suffered from priapism. Moreover, Natalia would have had to be vigilant not to smear the drawing with the side of her hand. In other words, she must have placed a sheet of blotting paper under her hand. This would have slowed the drawing process considerably.

I was at a loss. I couldn't possibly ask Natalia whether she had used blotting paper or not. Instead, I asked whether she'd like to tell me about the drawing process. It was an appropriate question, under the circumstances. I was hoping she would tell me she'd taken a photograph of the live model, because this would have saved her story. It would have allowed her to backpedal a little, and all would be well again.

But Natalia didn't want to tell me anything about the drawing process. She acknowledged my question with a sigh, as though drawing a picture of an erect penis with photographic precision was the most banal exercise in the world. Instead, she wanted to tell me the story of another significant hole in her childhood. The clock on her stomach told us there was enough time left, so she began.

"I was nine years old when I thought I'd found a body in the woods. I don't know about you, Doctor, but ever since I was a child I've been preparing for that day; I couldn't shake the thought that, at least once in my life, I would discover a body.

"I deliberately made my way to a stretch of terrain where I thought murderers might hide their victims. I walked across fields of heavy-going swampland, looking carefully at the ground as I went. Any colors that deviated from green, I interpreted as human body parts—especially when they were associated with forms that broke the harmony of the terrain. Could that be a finger hidden in the earth? Is that a piece of fabric from a jacket in the grass? My eyes have always been alert like this. Whenever I walked in the woods, my heart beat with a mixture of fear and excitement.

When I swam in the lakes, I was convinced that a body would soon come bobbing to the surface right in front of me.

"I can't really say where this expectation came from, because the very thought of a body slumped in a picturesque meadow or bloated with water both sickened and horrified me.

"Back then I devoured crime novels; children's books no longer held any interest for me. In the books I read, bodies were discovered in the cabins of cruise ships, in the beds of luxury hotels, in all kinds of closed, carefully guarded spaces. The murderers in these books always thought they had watertight alibis, that the clues they left behind would lead investigators on a wild-goose chase, and so they continued living their lives as though nothing had happened.

"But even as a child I had a tendency to believe that not all murderers moved in high society and not all of them were cold-blooded. I'd assumed—or perhaps read—that in real life there were murderers who committed murders in an impassioned frenzy, without premeditation. After the murder they were left with a big problem: what to do with the body. And it was these people, killed in a fit of rage and hidden in a hurry, that I expected to find.

"It was summer. I was playing with a friend on a steep hill covered in spruces and small bushes. The hillside sloped down toward a large, clear lake where we were going swimming, but before that we wanted to work up a good sweat. We wanted to be dirty, then succumb to the waters, we wanted to turn from hot to cold, then hot again, or at least I did. My friend did whatever I did or asked her to do.

"We skipped along the tracks trampled by animals' footsteps and carved out by the rains, sliding down along the sandy hillside. Our pants were full of sand. We climbed back up the hill and sprinted off again, sliding, crawling, wriggling, and the hot sand became glued to our skin. My friend knew perfectly well that she would get a thrashing when she arrived home. Her mother couldn't stand her children soiling their clothes; it went against her disciplinarian ideals. Many things that are an everyday part of my childhood, such as dirt, sent my friend's parents into a rage, so she and her older brother got a thrashing more often than not.

"I never actually saw rage flicker into life in her parents' eyes. But I was there once. Out of nowhere, there was a shout. My friend's name was hollered from the far end of the living room in such a tone that I ran away without saying goodbye. I went back home and warmed up the pot of gammon soup from the day before. In my own house I had the right to be hungry when I was hungry, but this right wasn't afforded my friend. I sat at the table slurping my soup straight from the pot. The broth formed a mesmerizing film of grease across my lips. It reminded me of when, as a younger child, I used to dip my fingertips in hot candle wax. Whenever I got the chance, I would make liquid forms set and tighten against my skin. I licked the grease from my lip or, in the case of candle wax, I would flick the hardened paraffin calluses from my fingertips. The film disappeared from my lips, and I wet them again. My fingers burned, but still I stuck them into the hot wax again and again. Of the grease films there was nothing left, but from my fingertips I was left with small wax cups the shape of a clock dial, little remnants that I arranged in crescent, rectangular or oval formations on the table. Nobody ever said to me 'Don't play with fire' or 'Don't play with your food.' I was able to arrange my wax fingertip cups and experiment with fatty lip gloss in peace and quiet—unlike my friend, who was in constant fear of spilling milk down her front.

"All this, and many other things besides, brought me unbridled joy. I named the feeling one of meticulousness. If my sense of joy was overwhelming, I would say aloud to myself: 'Goodness, how meticulous I feel.' Once I shared this feeling with my mother. 'Mother, I can feel the meticulousness here.' I rubbed my chest with the palm of my hand, for this was where my meticulousness resided, and my mother gave me an encouraging smile.

"If I was alone when I felt this meticulousness, and if I commented upon the matter out loud, I would nod to myself, as though I'd made a secret pact with the universe that it would take care of me, that it would ensure that my meticulousness wasn't rattled, no matter what happened. And if at that moment I had food in my mouth, as was often the case, I would smack my lips, demonstratively, in sync with the nodding of my head. A heavy nod, a wolverine smack of the lips, slowly, many times over, until I had finally swallowed all the food.

"This was my meticulousness.

"My friend would have been slapped on the spot if she'd behaved like this. Even as a child I realized how privileged I was because I could talk about whatever popped into my head without fear of punishment, I could smack my chops whenever we weren't sitting at the dinner table, when, naturally, I too was expected to behave properly. My parents would never have dreamed of smacking me. In this respect they were ahead of their time, unlike my friend's mother and father, for whom the boundaries of acceptable behavior seemed to narrow the older their children became.

"My friend, who was a year younger than me, was barely allowed to play with me at all. Apparently I was a bad influence on her. Once, we were separated from each other for a month, but then her parents realized she had no other friends but me. Her classmates avoided her like a leper, though there was nothing wrong with her physically. They left her out of their games as though she didn't exist. My friend accepted this, but her parents were startled. They rescinded their ban on us seeing each other and asked for me to come back. Our friendship still drove them to despair, but because they couldn't whip me they continued battering my friend instead.

"I never saw fear on my friend's face—or her brother's, for that matter. But I heard their cries. They were always beaten in the conservatory, and the windowpanes, which ran the length of the wall, did little to muffle their yelps.

"Didn't my friend's parents realize we could hear everything?

"Did they want their screaming children to serve as an example to the rest of us of what happens when you challenge the laws of the universe?

"Didn't they understand that my parents despised them and their brutal child-rearing methods?

"Despite everything, my friend was an impulsive creature,

just like me. She didn't want to spare a thought for the repercussions of her actions, but happily dirtied her clothes if such a thing was necessary for a game I had come up with.

"On the hillside, where we frolicked that hot summer's day, there was one particularly steep sandy verge, at the edge of which grew an ancient spruce tree. Soil erosion had revealed the tree's roots, formed in a magnificent, almost symmetrical structure like giant, rheumatic fingers on the keys of a piano. You could wrap your arms around those snake-like tentacles, knotted with bark, or dangle upside down with your legs around the trunk if you wanted to imagine the great lake as the sky or the great sky as a lake.

"That day I wanted to take my friend behind the roots, because there was no better hiding place in all the world. 'Want to slide down?' I asked her, then, without waiting for an answer, I jumped into the sand. I'd kicked my sandals off a moment ago, and now my feet sank into the hot sand up to the ankles.

"Once I had slid down to firmer ground, where my sandals awaited me, to the place where the roots dived beneath the earth, I stood up and turned.

"I saw my friend sliding toward me along the track I had left in the sand.

"I saw the roots and the sand.

"Out of the corner of my eye, I saw something in the wall of sand that looked like a dark, gleaming spot, something that most definitely didn't belong there.

"My friend slid down to where I stood, screaming with joy. I turned my head toward the gleaming spot and saw in the wall of sand, partially inside the sand, a woman's face, her mouth frozen in an agonized wail, her eyes wide open.

"I shouted.

"I shouted at the top of my voice, without holding back, without thinking.

" 'Body!' I shouted.

" 'Dead!' I shouted.

" 'Dead woman in the sand!' I shouted.

"At least, I should say, my mind shouted. It may well be that at that moment I gave a wordless shout, and that only my mind was thinking about the body, the cadaver, the dead woman in the sand.

"Hearing myself shout took me by surprise. I'd always been convinced that in a situation like this I wouldn't be one of the screamers. For a start, I was sure the realization of such a gruesome discovery would dawn on me a little bit at a time. First something would catch my eye, something from which I would draw initial conclusions, then I'd see a little more, gently move a piece of moss aside with my foot, just enough to make sure that what I saw in front of me was irrefutable evidence of death. A discovery in the cold water would be white, too, misshapen and bobbing upward, distorted by the water's surface. In my imagination things were always slightly hidden.

"Secondly, only rococo women in need of smelling salts would have screamed in a situation like this or gasped out a sigh intended as a scream from within the grip of their corsets. I was living in another time. I was born in the age of heroines, in the decade of fearless tomboys, and for this reason I assumed I would be able to remain resolutely silent. In my imagination my breathing certainly became faster—this I could do because I wasn't wearing any awkward clothing that prevented my chest from rising and falling. In my imagination I took a few calm steps back and committed the spot firmly to memory, and only then did I dash home to tell someone about my discovery because, after all, my shoes weren't made for standing around demurely; they were made for action.

"But now, in a single, bright, one-off glance, I noticed a dead woman's head and there seemed no end to my screams.

"I grabbed my sandals and hurtled into a barefoot run. I heard my friend start to scream too. She darted behind me, and we ran, we cried and shouted, from the top of the hillside all the way home.

"We went back to my house, of course, because my friend's father would have beaten her black and blue if we'd told him about our discovery. *You're lying!* he would have shouted at her, and I would have had to deal with everything by myself while my friend was out in the conservatory, her father's belt tanning her bare backside. So we started looking for my father and found him in the kitchen. He was sitting on a small stool, peeling potatoes into a basin. We were panting, out of breath, and eventually I managed to say: 'We found a woman buried in the sand! A dead woman!'

"My father immediately stood up to his full height. He was

swarthy and safe and unimaginably stable. I was sure he never had to tell himself out loud, 'Goodness, how meticulous I feel.' He was stability itself. He was always able to act in just the right way, and so he said: 'Come on, girls, let's take a look.'

"It wasn't hard to find the spot, because we knew the hillside like the back of our hand. The closer we got to the woman buried in the sand, the clearer my memories became.

"When I think of this episode now, I don't see events through my own eyes. I mean, I don't observe the surroundings as though through the subjective lens of a camera, first used in the history of cinema by Friedrich Wilhelm Murnau in his film *The Last Man.* You see, Doctor, how cleverly and logically I managed to slip in one of our supporting words, three in fact, the ones you collated last time? The last man. Imagine that.

"Murnau's silent film is superb. Have you seen it? The audience is forced to witness the agony in Emil Jannings's acting, the shame of the disgraced caretaker. The porter of a fine hotel is demoted to cleaning the men's bathrooms. He is shunned from society. He becomes a man without a role, a man without a uniform.

"One of the men in my memories, the one I called my last man last time, played the role of a wretch cheated by life so convincingly that eventually he became one. Nobody went out of their way to shun him; he managed to back himself into a dark corner and howl. In his youth he spilled his resentment onto paper. He harnessed his rage into a form of social analysis, extracted critique from his anger. He was a critic by profession, you see, until one day he ended up heckling full-time from his dark corner.

He continued to write critiques from time to time, once, twice a year, mostly cinema reviews, but he no longer critically assessed works of art—rather he practiced the art of anger, using artworks merely as conduits for his vituperations. And he always used the same words. That was his biggest mistake. His reviews lacked quality, and over time they became wholly predictable. But there was no point in telling him this. 'I'm just telling the truth, you bourgeois bitch!' he would simply shout back. That or, 'It's hardly my fault if society won't change no matter how much I critique it!' Back in the day, however, long, long ago, it was this man's writings that made me fall for him. When we first met, he had a permanent position as an assistant columnist at a newspaper. This excited me. Not his work, *per se*, and not his monthly salary, but the fact that he was able to put such ferocious words on display for everyone to read, and that he got paid for it. Back then there were plenty of people around to pat him on the back. And it felt as though they were patting me on the back too. I was young and gullible and stupid, even stupider than now. Believe me, Doctor, it really is possible to be stupider than I am today.

"Besides, I easily go crazy for people who know how to use the art of sublimation. Why might that be? Where have I learned a model for falling in love like this? My parents didn't use sublimation at all. A potato was just a potato, and that was that.

"For me, nothing is ever quite what it seems at first glance. A psychopath is not a psychopath, but the initial impetus behind a great story. A potato is not just a potato, but a symbol of the heaviness of existence: *Mutter, ich bin dumm!* Do you know that film, Doctor? *The Turin Horse?* The characters are always eating potatoes. Nothing but potatoes. When I now think about my father, sitting on a stool, peeling potatoes into a basin, I can't stop myself from becoming emotional: the perpetuity of potatoes, their beauty and simplicity . . . the automated movements of the thumb and peeling knife . . . It was hypnotic. Heaviness and lightness all at once. I loved life, because it was my father's fingers—not my fingers—that skillfully twisted the potato peels away so that I could run around freely outside.

"Where was I? Yes, my father, my friend and I arrived at the sandy verge. I can still see the three of us as if from the outside. I can see my own fair-haired figure, but it's blurred, as though someone had quickly sketched me: approximate, something like that. My friend was a thickly plaited head of blond hair, nothing more. She had no gaze; she was a silent witness, unable to tell anyone anything in her own words.

"My father, however, was full sized.

"My father had a face, a spectrum of expressions.

"My father looked at me quizzically, not suspiciously but more out of curiosity. He was tense, though not as tense as the act of finding a body in the sand might have presupposed.

"At that moment I realized that he didn't believe we'd made such a discovery. And because my father was my rock, my meticulous foundation, my own belief in our story started running through my fingers like sand. I looked at my father, and all of a sudden I was certain that whatever we had found, it wasn't the body of a woman.

"But what had we found?

"I leaned against the largest root in the cluster, which had grown tight against the wall of sand, the place where I had seen a dark, gleaming spot out of the corner of my eye. Sunlight struck the spot, which shone just as it had before, and I understood: a face cannot gleam like that, living or dead.

"I showed my father the spot. He could take care of the rest, that's why he'd come out to the hillside in the first place.

"My father took a step past me and started laughing. 'It's a mask,' he said. 'Someone was having fun and buried the mask in the hillside!' He stepped closer to the spot and pressed his hand into the sand.

"But it wasn't a mask. It was a magazine. A pornographic magazine that someone had carefully hidden. Someone had hidden the magazine's very essence, making its flat surface curved and mask-like. Someone had gone to a lot of trouble to turn that magazine into a dead woman buried in the sand.

"But the woman in the picture was not dead. Her mouth was open, and in her mouth was an enormous penis. Her eyes were open, she looked like she was about to choke.

"My father chuckled, his expression smug. I laughed too, giggled uncontrollably. The laughter soon passed to my friend. This really was something to laugh about! And we laughed; boy, how we laughed. My father smiled, amused, but with not a hint of gloating. Another father might have teased us, but my father wasn't that kind of man.

"I was already trying to form words to tell my mother about

our adventure. I was planning on telling her about the adult magazine in the same way that adults spoke to me about adult drinks, and I wanted to make her laugh. Because if my mother laughed, I would be able to accept the fact that I hadn't had the courage to approach the gleaming spot myself. If my mother began to chuckle after hearing this story, I could live with the fact that because of my own cowardice my friend and I had missed the opportunity to get our hands on a phenomenal secret. Maybe it was a good thing that my father pulled the magazine out of the sand. If the magazine had ended up in my hands or those of my friend, we would have had to keep quiet about it. As important as such secrets are to children, they are also oppressive matters. Their importance is in direct correlation with their oppressiveness, and not every child is capable of bearing such weight. I had no way of knowing whether my friend would have the necessary strength when it came to the crunch. Would she have blabbed about the living-dead woman with the penis in her mouth to her mother and father, taken another thrashing and in doing so cowardly release herself from the pressure of our secret?

"My father picked up the magazine, and we set off back to the house. He went into the sauna, where he started burning the magazine in the stove.

"Smoke rose from the sauna chimney, so I believe he really did burn it."

And so ended Natalia's story of the second significant hole in her childhood. I was speechless. The ease with which Natalia had inserted every one of the supporting words I had given her—

and even an entire noun phrase—shocked me. My other clients, to whom I had assigned the same exercise, always made sure I knew when they were using a word I had suggested. They paused slightly before the word, then enunciated it clearly, and paused again before continuing their story. One client even interrupted the story altogether and started talking at length about alternative plots and subplots that had come to mind at each word but that were ultimately rejected. It was one of these rejected ideas that turned into the most significant conversation of that particular session; this is one method of precipitating collaborative layering. Natalia, meanwhile, only made a meal out of the words "hole," "promise" and "the last man." The remaining seven words flowed into the story like droplets of water into a rain barrel.

If I hadn't had the word list in my lap and a pen in my hand, if I hadn't been as alert as I was, the entire purpose of our session would have disappeared as though it had never existed.

I stared in bewilderment at my list, where, to pass the time, waiting for the words to appear, I'd made notes of my own. The French maxim, which I had written around the supporting words, is, for what it's worth, one I am particularly fond of. I love puns and tongue twisters on religious themes, but there aren't really any good examples in Finnish. Other languages aren't much better either. In the French, this *jeu de mots* is ingenious, the great fisherman (*le grand pêcheur*) becoming the great sinner (*le grand pécheur*) simply by cutting the circumflex in half and creating an acute accent, in other words by changing only a tiny detail of the spelling. The closest I can think of is if a great singer became a great sinner, or vice versa, but that's nowhere near as elegant, and when there is a lack of elegance, as is often the case with our crude witticisms, everything is wrong. For example, *If Moses supposes his toeses are roses, then Moses supposes erroneously, for nobody's toeses are posies or rosies, as Moses supposes his toeses to be.* I hardly have to tell you what I think of such facile nonsense.

∅

~~hole~~

~~promise~~

secret

~~blue-and-red~~

Grand pêcheur   ~~black-and-white~~   devant l'Éternel

~~transparent~~

~~home~~

scream

jam

~~the last man~~

By any logic, Natalia's exquisite display of word usage should have brought me an immense sense of joy. After all, she had done precisely as I'd asked, only far more thoroughly than I had imagined. Nonetheless, something was bothering me. I couldn't sense any pain in her story, neither past nor present. Her stories were too full, too precise and smooth, too complete.

And I realized that Natalia had done her best to make sure I remained a passive listener. Her questions, such as *Perhaps I was back then, as I am now, completely emotionally transparent*, were purely rhetorical. She didn't wait for my reaction but hurried on instead. Even when her questions were addressed to me directly, such as *Do you mind if we return to this drawing later?*, she barely waited to hear my melodious hum of consent, that rising sound familiar from all psychodynamic therapy, a sound meant to encourage the speaker to delve deeper into the subject at hand.

And so we found ourselves in classic emotional displacement territory. Part of my professional skill set is being able to see this and beyond. My job is to incrementally allow transference to become a part of the layering process, just as I do in traditional in-and-out therapy sessions. My initial hypothesis, which I needed to adjust surprisingly little through the course of her therapy, was the following: Natalia's almost supernatural need to enchant me with her stories was in direct correlation with the problems of her sexual life. Superficially, therefore, her diagnosis was an F52.7 or hypersexuality, also known as nymphomania. But when I scratched the surface, which beneath my calm exterior I was frantically trying to do all the while, a number of other issues arose: a disguised fear of encounters, a fear of allowing oneself to be swept up in the moment with another person. In other words, Natalia went through both men and words as a way of masking her own vulnerability.

We would have to continue the exercises.

I glanced at the clock on Natalia's stomach. According to the clock, we had three minutes left. I looked at my own digital watch, which used a server based in Frankfurt-am-Main, which in turn took the time from an atomic clock—and not just any atomic clock, but the meteorological primary clock, which might lose up to one second every hundred million years. The watch was given to me by a fantastically rich client, not the poet who gave me the anthologies, but a major shareholder in a gaming company. This client had exceptionally weak impulse control, a matter that manifested itself in the gifts she gave me in bursts of generosity. According to my watch, we had two minutes and twenty-three seconds left.

Natalia was lying silently on the couch. It seems she was waiting for her alarm clock to start rattling, that and perhaps to hear some compliments on how excellently she had completed the exercise.

I joined her in silence.

The clock ticked loudly.

With each tick, there was less time left, and in reality there was even less because, as I mentioned, Natalia's clock was slow.

When by my clock we had only one minute and sixteen seconds left, Natalia suddenly opened her mouth.

"Listen. Just so you don't think that everything that's wrong with me, all these deviations . . . so you don't think it's all because of those pornographic women with their mouths open. That's not it at all. I have plenty of stories. Goodness, if only you knew. And there is one childhood experience of holes that was entirely positive; erotic but not pornographic. A memory from an illustrated encyclopedia of animals.

"In the picture, a female tortoise was giving birth to a large white egg in a pit she'd dug in the sand. That birth, that laying of the egg. Goodness. I never tired of that picture. That wonderful, smooth white egg making its way out of the back of her shell, from that stretched hole surrounded by scaly skin, hanging eagerly toward the ground from the weight of the egg. That's right, the egg came out of the tortoise's pussy as if from a leather sheath. Slowly. Slowly. I have no idea whether laying the egg caused the tortoise pain. I wanted to imagine that it gave the tortoise immense pleasure. There were countless eggs in the sandpit. They were like golf balls. Something about them excited me, their abundance, the manner of their production. The smoothness of the shells, the uniform quality, and the fact that they came out so slowly. That they came out, just like that. That they had only one direction, instead of moving back and forth in perpetuity. That, if anything, was meticulous!"

Natalia fell silent. A moment passed, then according to my clock it was exactly 14:00 hours. I began straightening my legs but didn't speak a word until Natalia's clock started rattling. By my watch it was 14:00:37.

Above the sound of the clock, I almost shouted a *Well*, but this time Natalia switched the clock off immediately.

"You really have considered your relationship to pornography," I began. "Last time we tried to build a foundation for today's session by using the themes of 'men,' 'rape,' 'pussy,' and 'shoving into the pussy' as key words. Today you've given a detailed account of women's mouths, men's erections and a tortoise's vagina. Excellent work!"

I didn't wait for Natalia's reaction, because I wanted to give my suggestion for the topic of our next session quickly. "Shall we continue with the same subject area? We didn't have time for a proper discussion today, so shall we reserve our next session for some post-exercise discussion and analysis?"

As I spoke, I suddenly had a magnificent idea, one that I gasped out without giving it a second thought: "To stimulate our minds, we could consider the painting on the wall! You are very familiar with this painting, isn't that right? As I'm sure you remember, the work is called *Ear-Mouth*. So, we shall continue with holes, but next time we will concentrate on communication, on the anatomy of listening and speaking. How does that sound?"

Natalia was already standing. She was shaking her wrists, as though they had been put through their paces in the course of our session. "Yes, by all means," she said flatly, then slung her handbag over her shoulder and walked into the hallway. I followed her out.

In shaking her hand, I tried to hand back her sketch of the penis, but she gave me a disparaging look, an ocean of disappointment in her eyes. "You can keep it," she said eventually, then her mouth melted into a smile and she walked out the door.

RECOVERY PROGRAM
WEEK 3

Instruction: No instructions.
Free analysis of the thoughts that arose during the pornography exercise.
Au style de Bouchoreille, a.k.a. Ear-Mouth.

Though we were only in the initial phases of the rehabilitation process, the presence of the painting on my wall was beginning to make me impatient. There it hung, its radiant glory filling the room, but to my astonishment, after our initial session Natalia hadn't paid it the slightest attention. Not even a glance, let alone any passing comments that might have led us naturally into a conversation about the canvas and the strange coincidence that Natalia's grandmother had owned it until the mid-1990s—if, that is, Natalia was telling the truth. And it was a conversation we needed to have, because if *Ear-Mouth* really had once belonged to Natalia's family, it followed that this must be the reason she had come to my office in the first place. But why? Getting to the bottom of this was of the utmost importance.

Natalia arrived for our third meeting wearing a gold-speckled woolen sweater. It was apparent that she had chosen the sweater to fit the color scheme of *Ear-Mouth*, and this I took as a positive signal given the subject of today's session. That notwithstanding, I decided to steer our conversation toward the painting indirectly, because I was still pondering the questions brought up in our previous session.

In now-familiar fashion, Natalia lay down on the couch and placed the alarm clock on her stomach. Given that its four legs were thin and spindly, it remained upright surprisingly well on its soft surface, constantly rising and falling in time with Natalia's breathing.

"So," I began. "Thank you again for last week. What kind of feelings did telling stories about holes bring up for you?"

Natalia ran a finger along the clock's right-hand bell, raised like one of Mickey Mouse's ears. "Feelings? Well," she said somewhat reluctantly, as though the matter had already been comprehensively dealt with, though we hadn't really touched upon it at all. "I guess I'm surprised at how much pornography interested me when I was younger. And how little it interests me today."

Natalia reached out her other hand toward the clock too. She gently placed her forefinger and middle finger on the left-hand bell, pressed both thumbs against the clock face and began to explain. "Nowadays I don't resort to pornography made by other people. At some point it started to bore me profoundly. It doesn't arouse me anymore. If one of my lovers wants to watch a video with me, that's fine; I have plenty. A long time ago I ordered reams of VHS tapes on the subject. That was before DVDs had become commonplace. You see, I didn't find sex a problem; rather

I was living in a state of innocence. I found everything exciting. I tried to get hold of all different kinds of genres: gonzo, fisting, red rhapsody . . . Japanese *hamedori*, *bukkake* and *futanari* porn . . . movies about fetishes, dominatrices, candaulism . . . Depictions of very niche sexual practices, erotic hirsutism or Tales of the Unwashed Anushka. Nothing really sick, and nothing illegal, of course. I just wanted to understand different tastes, and I wanted to find out whether any particular subgenre might meet my own interests."

"And did you find your own interests?" I managed to ask, not because Natalia's sexual proclivities interested me *per se*, but because, yet again, I saw another possible key to her underlying problems.

As was to be expected, Natalia had used her video collection to undertake a journey of self-discovery. "I like penises, so I quickly realized that gay porn was my thing," she began in a teacherly voice, as though she had been through the same details with someone else before me. "Moreover, I like gay porn for the simple reason that it's harder to fake than traditional straight porn. When a man being anally penetrated finally ejaculates, it's real, it's something you can't pretend."

Natalia paused to assess her words.

"Don't get me wrong; men sometimes have to fake it too, especially if they have ejaculated a lot in a short space of time and they're running low on the goods. Then the studios use fake sperm, made of confectioners' sugar and water. But fundamentally I want to believe that the men in these movies, and the men in my life, don't fake anything. I want to believe that their enjoyment is real."

I was reminded of Natalia's drawing of the penis, for which she claimed to have taken inspiration "first from pictures, then from a live model." And when I thought of that veiny, black-and-white member, sketched in pencil, I realized that her description of the genesis of the drawing might well have been true *à la lettre*. If the man who agreed to her bizarre request was young, healthy and virile, he would doubtless have been able to get his member up time and again for Natalia to draw, as long as she rewarded him at regular intervals. And why wouldn't she? After all, by her own admission, she loved penises.

"I like stories too," Natalia continued. "And stories are born from hierarchies. For this reason, I've never been remotely interested in watching two equally muscular men or two bears screwing each other. It's just monotonous pumping—yawn! I'm more of the master-apprentice school myself. And I'm not alone; there are enough films in this style to last a lifetime. An army recruit is making his bed, an officer dashes in to help him. Boarding schools, children's homes . . . homes, even . . . I don't mean to shock you, my dear doctor, but in these stories the 'daddies' sometimes even teach their own sons a lesson or two. Therapists screw their patients. It's a classic scenario, the eroticization of the taboo. But it's all fiction. Everything except the ejaculation. Except when they need to bring out the confectioners' sugar, that is."

I noted she seemed to assume that stories of incest would shock me, though such material has been at the heart of psychoanalysis ever since the time of Freud. Perhaps she was simply taunting me. Surely this much she must know about the history of psycho-analysis. It is on these very principles that my own methods are based. My theories simply take impetus from the artistic creative force found in each and every one of us.

Natalia's fascination for homosexual pornography was an interesting detail. From research literature, I've learned that women who have problems with their own femininity often idealize eroticism between men. Those who have difficulty taking control of their own internal space are particularly susceptible to fantasies of this nature. Freud spoke of penis envy, and sometimes not even the most brazen and self-aware individuals can avoid it. Individuals just like Natalia.

A few years ago, I had a client who was a famous feminist. She came to my office specifically to work on "the problematics of her internal space," as she put it. What she found problematic was that she was unable to achieve an orgasm with her husband unless she was riding on top of him. Whenever she felt the urge to throw herself like a smoldering ember upon a wave of submission, she had to imagine that her husband's penis was hers and that her vagina was her husband's. Such a feat of mental gymnastics was only possible in the riding position. I asked her what the problem was. If this little fantasy brought her unbridled pleasure, why try to suppress it? The woman was stubborn. She was convinced there was a sadistic misogynist lurking somewhere inside her, and together we began the process of tracing it. Toward the end of her therapy, she successfully found within herself an extremely

adaptable old-school chauvinist who time and again tried to sabo-
tage her exemplary work for women's equality. The client eventually managed to destroy the "wanker chameleon" (as she named
her discovery) on the rug in my office by stamping to smithereens
Lynyrd Skynyrd's live album *One More from the Road*, a vinyl LP
she had acquired in the division of her late father's estate. After
this episode, she was once again able to ride her husband without
the pangs of a guilty conscience.

Natalia removed her hand from the clock and sat up abruptly.
"May I use that blanket on the chair? I'm cold." Without waiting
for an answer, she stood up, snatched the blanket, opened it and
pulled it over herself as she lay down again. The clock, like her
hands, was hidden beneath it.

"Even the smuttiest gay porn eventually leaves you numb.
And watching videos by yourself gets boring after a while. But
who could I watch them with? Most of my male friends find the
idea of sodomy wholly intolerable. All of a sudden they become
terribly moralistic. Of course. They can't bear the thought of
someone entering *them*, penetrating *them*, though they think it's
perfectly normal to imagine penetrating a teenage girl. I recently
read a research paper showing that the most typical pornography
search terms men type into Google are *anal, money shot, teen, braces*
and *school uniform*. As long as the backside is a teenage girl's backside and the penis their own imaginary penis, everything is fine.
Breathtaking double standards, don't you think?"

For the first time in the course of this session, I noted a hint
of emotion in Natalia's voice. "It seems that way," I agreed, shar-

ing her irritation, then tried to gather up her disparate strands of thought. "You said that porn no longer interests you and that you sometimes watch videos with your male lovers. At their instigation, I take it? And something besides homosexual pornography. What does that feel like?"

This question, aimed at pushing the conversation forward, and which is structurally very similar to the questions I pose in so-called in-and-out therapy sessions, was met with an irritated scoff.

"Well, of course I don't watch them *with* my lovers. After all, I've already seen them. The lover watches, I observe his reaction. That can be arousing sometimes."

There was more than a hint of condescension in Natalia's voice. She wanted to make it clear to me that pornography was beneath her nowadays.

"You see, I've lost my innocence in this regard too, Doctor. If on occasion, just as an experiment, I am home alone and decide to slide a VHS into my ancient video player, I soon begin to imagine things that aren't on the screen. The actors' breaks, for instance. Bathroom breaks, tea breaks, toast breaks, breaks to stretch their legs. Did you know that, during filming, the exact positions of the actors' feet are marked on the floor with tape? That way the actors can return to precisely the same positions once they come back from their breaks. These are the kinds of things I think about these days whenever I watch professionals screwing each other. Pieces of tape used to maintain the illusion of reality."

I imagined Natalia sitting cross-legged in front of a large TV screen watching scene after scene of intercourse, looking for continuity errors and writing them down in a notebook. It was a desolate image, and Natalia's voice was by now so icy that I thought it best to move on to the subject of *Ear-Mouth*.

"I understand. You've had enough of pornography and your mind starts to look for new sources of stimulus. Ultimately pornography always leaves people in a state of dissatisfaction, whereas art, or so I believe, can give us a deep sense of joy time and again. Like the painting hanging above you, for instance. It stirs me every time I step into the room."

I tried to keep my voice steady as I performed this shift, though my heart was beating so fast that my words almost cracked. "So, *Ear-Mouth* belonged to your grandmother a long time ago? Your father's mother, I believe you said. It's quite a coincidence that you and the painting are now right here in the same room again. Or what do you think?"

I acquired *Ear-Mouth* at Bukowski's auction house in late 2001. Or was it early 2002? It was around the time when our country abandoned the mark and adopted the euro. At first I was at a loss with the new currency. In order to truly understand the value of any item, everything had to be multiplied by 5.95, and you had to keep that large sum—or value—in mind, alongside the tiny-looking sum in euros, until you made a decision to buy.

To this day I still don't know the exact price of *Ear-Mouth* as the hammer came down. I still have a receipt for it, of course, but it's not so important that I feel the need to go down to my basement and rake through age-old Mercantil folders to find it.

Instead, as quickly as possible I needed an answer to a question that had been bothering me from the start, namely whether Natalia's story about the connection between her grandmother and *Ear-Mouth* was true or false. Furthermore, did I have reason to believe any of Natalia's stories at all?

I decided to proceed with caution in my investigations. *Il n'y a pas le feu*, as they say, *hold your horses*. And so I controlled myself, though the stall of my soul was engulfed in flames. I didn't immediately start inquiring as to what kind of woman could have given birth to Natalia's father, the man for whom a potato was just a potato, the man who fathered a girl for whom nothing was as it first appeared. What kind of personality could have given rise to a man who, to all intents and purposes, settled for very little and for whom life itself was enough (in contrast to Natalia and, it would appear, her grandmother)? A person for whom life itself is enough would never have bought a painting like this.

I suppose at this juncture I should tell those of you not acquainted with the painting's artistic and historical background that *Bouchoreille* or *Ear-Mouth* is a painting by Elise Watteauville dating from 1979. Does this name sound familiar? It is hardly surprising if it doesn't ring any bells, as Elise W. disappeared from the Finnish art scene during the recession years without so much as a trace. It would appear she'd had enough of our bleak country and decided to flee abroad, specifically to France—being a Finnish-French artist as she was. Then again, perhaps it would be more correct to call her Franco-Finnish. According to Bukowski's catalogue raisonnée, she was born in Aire-sur-la-Lys in 1948, so surely she must be Franco-Finnish. Her mother was Finnish, her father French, and she learned both languages.

But did she learn Finnish first? Her mother must have spoken to her far more than her father did, as was the norm back then; mothers cooed to their babies while fathers simply grunted, and in that sense Finnish would undoubtedly have been her first language, a matter that ought to make her a Finnish-French artist, regardless of where she resided.

Some may think this is splitting hairs: Finnish-French, Franco-Finnish, what's the difference? But to me words are not inconsequential. Words, and indeed their sequence in relation to other words, affect everything; besides, language is what my clients and I primarily work with. Or should I say we work *through* language? No, perhaps not. Not at all! We operate *in* language just as a competitive swimmer competes *in* the water, like a bird flies *in* the air, a worm burrows *in* the earth and a tree burns *in* flames. And because language is our element, it would be irresponsible of me if I didn't correct and update it whenever possible.

Giving the matter proper consideration, I feel convinced that French must have been Elise's primary language after all. The primary language and the mother tongue can sometimes be different. For most people, such as myself, they are one and the same thing, but in families that operate with two or more languages, these languages generally end up fulfilling different functions. Different languages meet different needs, and beneath different languages different thoughts can swim.

It is abundantly clear that in Aire-sur-la-Lys, Elise would have had to use French with everybody except her mother. In Aire-sur-la-Lys, Finnish would have been a secret language, a strange jumble of sounds, an umbilical cord wound around the neck, a phonetic asylum all of its own, *un couloir de la mort*. If Elise's parents had wanted (as I'm sure they did) their daughter's linguistic and thereby also her emotional development to progress from cooing and cawing to a world of fully formed concepts and ideas, they would have spoken lots of French to her and only a small amount of Finnish.

We can therefore consider Elise Watteauville *une artiste franco-finlandaise*. Her parents divorced when she was sixteen years old. After attending the *lycée*, Elise moved back to Finland with her mother and began studying at the Pori Art School. Due to her exceptional talents, she progressed to the Ateneum in Helsinki only a year later.

Elise spent her summers in Ontojoki, where according to Bukowski's catalogue her mother's family originated, until in 1975 she moved there permanently and continued to live there for almost another twenty years. As someone who grew up at the same time, I hazard that Elise moved to the countryside in an attempt to escape the overly politicized artistic circles in the capital into which she had blithely slipped after her studies. Circles like these can easily gnaw away at a person's motivation, unless their mind is one hundred percent dogmatic or one hundred and ten percent opportunistic.

In the south, Elise had a wonderful future ahead of her. In this context I refuse outright to use the conditional perfect tense, which the ear might automatically thrust into a situation like this, because I don't want to dilute Elise's wonderful future by adding a hint of conditionality or uncertainty. Elise was on the brink of a magnificent breakthrough, period. The catalogue raison-née tells us as much. The academic years 1972–1973–1974 were a period of unparalleled success. Elise's vividly colorful collages were selected for an exhibition of young artists at the Kunsthalle Helsinki. She was the recipient of the Dukaatti Prize awarded by the Finnish Art Association. The Sara Hildén Museum acquired Elise's environmentally conscious gouache painting *Oil on Canvas* for its own collections.

But then came 1975, when at the age of twenty-seven Elise moved back to Ontojoki, where she was surrounded by cows, sheep, fields and meadows, alone, alone, alone.

When I look at *Ear-Mouth* up close, I think I can make out a shard of a broken heart. It's there in the lower left-hand corner of the canvas. It's hard to find, and when reproduced on paper—as in the auction brochure where I initially found the work—it's impossible to see it. But when the painting is right in front of your eyes, when you look at it from only a few inches away, one of the swirls of paint is shaped almost exactly like half a broken heart; half a little flower, magenta and bell-shaped, the kind that grow in their dozens along the stalks of the ornamental plant *Dicentra spectabilis*, and which, as a child, I used to tug loose and tear into pieces.

Could Elise have left a clue in the painting as to the real reason behind her sudden departure?

Ear-Mouth is divided along a slight diagonal into two sections. The left side of the canvas is textured with pigments ground into a powder: northern Italian umbra and celadonite and two different types of slate originally from the Dolomites. The right side of the canvas is textured with soil pigments: okra, iron oxides, earthy greens. The right half is more granular than the left, with the exception of the roughness of the broken heart on the left-hand side; here Elise left the soil pigments coarse. In the middle of the canvas hangs the central image of the work: the glowing, almost translucent ear-mouth itself, which Elise has painted in a *tempera grassa* solution. As if to underline the impression of an Orthodox icon, she has surrounded the contours of the ear-mouth with gold leaf.

The minute my eye fell on *Ear-Mouth* in the Bukowski catalogue, I called the auction house and reserved a bidding number. I didn't dare make an advance bid, because I was worried I would lose the painting to someone else. Though *Ear-Mouth* looked like the kind of work that many people wouldn't give as much as a second glance and that most would walk past either indifferently or with a mild sense of disgust, I was convinced that there were others in this world like me, people who would instantly understand the significance of the work.

Eventually, the act of acquiring the painting for myself was relatively straightforward. Was its value five thousand euros or thirty thousand marks, five thousand marks or thirty thousand euros? I have no idea. But I acquired it, and I haven't regretted my decision once.

"Well, my grandmother knew the artist's grandmother. They were both from the same village," Natalia began her account. "Back then her daughter, the artist, Mademoiselle W, as we called her, lived in Ontojoki. She painted *Ear-Mouth* in a barn that she had converted into a studio. That's where my grandmother bought the work, straight out of the barn. The paint had barely dried."

"Did you live there too?" I asked, but Natalia continued talking over me.

"I spent my childhood in the neighboring parish. There were countless villages in the area. Small, some with only a few families, some slightly larger, then the village with the church, my village."

Natalia pulled back the blanket with a single swipe of the hand. "Actually, many of the place names near our village are rather naughty-sounding. There's Paskolampi, Hevonperseen-mutka, Kivesjärvi—just imagine living on the shores of 'Lake Testes'! What on earth were people thinking when they came up with names like that? I assume *paska* probably referred to a brown, muddy pond, and *hevonperse* must have meant a very remote place, the butt-end of nowhere perhaps, and not a literal horse's ass. Be that as it may, as a child these names titillated me immensely. Nobody could chide me for swearing or misbehaving; I was just reading the map. I was invincible! One day I picked up the map and marched into the kitchen, where my mother was baking a cake. I ran my finger along the contours of the landscape, the hills, roads, the power cables. When I found what I was looking for, I stabbed my finger at the name and cried out: Mulkkusaaret—

'Dick Island'! Now, now, my mother said, but her voice was soft, almost mischievous. As though we'd both decided that, on this one occasion, the responsibility for my using naughty words lay somewhere else, in the earthy, masculine mouths of a bygone age . . ."

In Natalia's voice there was suddenly a sense of defiant pride in her homeland. Over the years this is something I have become very familiar with, after listening to clients from the boondocks. People with a keen curiosity leave the countryside behind and head for the big cities; this has always been the case and will always remain so. It's as if they imagine that, in the name of some cosmic equilibrium and sense of justice, the metropolis should make up for perceived wrongs by granting them maximum happiness. But over time, even Natalia's heart had begun to warm to the landscape of her childhood with its cracked bitumen roads and dilapidated gas-station bars.

"What about your grandmother?" I interrupted. "Where did she live?"

"My grandmother spent her final years in the nearby town, next door to her new gentleman friend. She had a one-bedroom apartment of about fifty square meters; that's where I moved once I'd finished middle school. I couldn't stand my home or the village anymore, and I didn't want to go to our local high school as there were nasty rumors going around about the math teacher. I got to spend the majority of my time in the one-bedroom apartment by myself. To all intents and purposes, my grandmother lived with the man she loved."

Natalia remained still, thinking about this for a moment, perhaps pondering those last words, the mystery of living with a
man you actually loved. Some people can do it, for others it will
always be impossible. But this is not the direction in which Natalia decided to steer her story.

"My mother called her mother-in-law every day and tried to
fish for gossip about me. She was incredibly worried. Like the other
teenagers, I'd started having sex in high school, generally during
my free periods. I started drinking too. But my grandmother was
a shrewd lady. In the version of events she told my mother, she left
certain things out, though she knew almost everything there was
to know. She believed adventure was a part of youth; after all, she
had had plenty of adventures during the war."

At this point Natalia chose not to specify precisely what she
was getting up to in those adventures between her own bedroom
and someone else's bedroom, between the high school building
and another building, drunk or sober, or what her grandmother
had got up to during the Winter War, the Continuation War and,
no doubt, in the interwar years too. I could easily imagine those
first boyfriends, the wartime romances, and the eternal worry
that troubles a mother's heart.

"So your grandmother was an art lover?"

"Yes."

"Did she collect works of art?"

"Yes."

"And she bought a work by a local girl?"

"Yes."

"And what do you think of *Ear-Mouth*?"

Natalia began to recount the story. The painting used to hang in her grandmother's living room. It was different from the other paintings her grandmother owned, which were all far more conservative. Winter landscapes, summer landscapes, moon-lit scenes, floral still lifes, standard, murky grandma material, heavy green-brown wall hangings and kitschy, glittering angels. But *Ear-Mouth* was a work by a local girl, and in 1979 that local girl found herself in a spot of financial trouble. And because in their village people were in the habit of working together for the greater good, to the point of excess, her grandmother had bought the painting still wet.

"My grandmother never told me whether she actually liked *Ear-Mouth*," Natalia said after a short pause. "I assume she did, because she hung it in pride of place, though the painting didn't suit the rest of the interior at all."

I realized it was best to remain silent, though Natalia held regular pauses. I sensed she was about to answer my question, and I was right.

"That painting meant so much to me," she whispered. "And it was the only one of my grandmother's paintings that had any monetary value in the years after the recession, when she needed some money. Or rather, when I needed some money. I was up to my ears in debt. I'd been ordering little things through postal retail catalogues, different-colored PVC pants, jewelry, videos, all kinds of useless junk, and the bills were piling up. Don't ask how or why. I don't have an answer. I'm not that person anymore."

Natalia took a deep breath and prepared to tell me the thing that, deep down, she knew she would have to tell me today.

"You can guess what happened. Yes, my dear grandmother wanted to help me. She sold the painting for my benefit, so that I could sort out my finances and start college with a clean slate. It was terrible. That painting was the only thing I'd hoped to inherit one day. No other object held any significance for me. As a child, the image in that painting became seared into my soul. Back then my grandmother lived in her own detached house, only a few blocks from our house. She offered me cinnamon cookies and warmed milk, and I whispered my secrets to the ear in the painting, blew sugarcoated kisses at the painting's mouth. Even now, as I look up and see *Ear-Mouth*'s ear and mouth floating diagonally above me, I can almost taste the hot, watery, sweet milk in my mouth, feel the rough surface of the cookies against my tongue."

Natalia sat up to take a sip from the sports bottle she had placed next to the couch. The bottle was transparent and had a straw that flipped up at the top and extended down into the bottle. Though the bottle looked full of water, it made a strong slurping sound when she took a sip.

"I was ready to do any kind of work for a year or so, even as a call girl if necessary, to get my money situation in order. Anything to keep the painting in the family. But when I heard about the sale, I couldn't do anything, not even cry, because my grandmother was only thinking of my own good."

There was no longer any room for doubt. Natalia had known "Mademoiselle W," though Watteauville's name doesn't appear on the front of the canvas. She was also able to place the artist in the village of Ontojoki and the genesis of the painting in the barn. There was no doubt in my mind that Natalia had come to my office specifically because of that painting. Somehow, she had been able to establish *Ear-Mouth*'s chain of ownership—but how? Bukowski's auction house would certainly never give out buyers' details without written permission. And what exactly did Natalia want? Did she want to buy the painting back from me?

"I know what you're thinking," Natalia said quietly. "But it's only half the truth. I really do need help. I'm not making up my problems. And I don't want to talk about that painting again. I don't even want to see it! I loved my grandmother. She was only thinking of my future when she sold it. When I think about this, it hurts so much it feels like something's ripping me apart inside. I couldn't have imagined this, but now that I'm sitting here looking at it, talking about it, I almost wish I could die. Do you under-stand me in the slightest? There inside its frame, that painting holds everything I could never talk to people about as a child. I am *Ear-Mouth*. What I mean is, *Ear-Mouth* is the side of me that even as a child had too much to hide. Well. I'll stop now before I implode right here on the spot."

After a moment's silence, Natalia spluttered loudly, as though hurriedly returning to the surface after diving too deep. After this she could no longer contain her sobs. And so began an unbri-dled weeping, an inconsolable wailing that rose from a bottom-less pit of distress, the kind that cannot be calmed with merely a few comforting words.

I stood up and offered her a tissue, a box of which I always kept on my desk for situations like this. She took one, crushed it in her fist and continued bawling, stopping only to catch her breath. I went to the small kitchen to fetch her a glass of water, though of course I remembered that her own water bottle was propped next to the couch. But there's something deeply soothing about handing someone a glass of water. It's a small, caring gesture with which I let the client know that they're not alone with their demons.

While I was fetching the water, Natalia had rolled onto her side and turned to face the wall, her knees pulled up against her chest. Her entire body was shivering as though with a fever, when suddenly something extraordinary happened. I saw a misty, turquoise aura around her body, an inch or so from her skin. I swear that's what I saw. I blinked in disbelief and the turquoise disappeared, only to reappear, refracted in front of me, slightly displaced from its original position, as if it was now glued to Natalia's body. Then the hue disappeared for good.

At that point I did something I had never done before in my career as a therapist, something that will never happen again in this room. I acted as though in a trance. I placed the glass on the table, sat down on the couch next to Natalia and gently stroked her side. "Natalia," I whispered. "Everything will be fine. We don't need to talk about the painting again. I can take *Ear-Mouth* down and prop it over there, facing the wall. Everything will be just fine, I promise."

I'm not partial to superstition, in my reality spoons do not bend of their own accord, but now I felt like I was witnessing a great mystery. Throughout my body I sensed the potent fate binding Natalia and *Ear-Mouth* together. Common sense rebuked me, *nonsense*, but my basal ganglia wouldn't listen. From the deepest recesses of the brain stem, hidden in the caudate nucleus, came a voice, deeper than the voice of reason but far, far more powerful, and it whispered to me: *Ear-Mouth brought Natalia to you . . .*

It's hard to explain all this, though I've subsequently been through the situation with my mentor many times. After all, this wasn't the first time I'd watched a visceral outburst of sorrow on my couch. In my office I have witnessed all kinds of reactions, shouting, beating of cushions, what have you, but it doesn't normally affect me so profoundly. And yet there I sat, my hand on my client's side, humming through one of my favorite nursery rhymes. After a while the words came back to me too, and I began singing of a squirrel lying sweetly in his home of moss. My stroking hand and singing voice gradually found a shared rhythm, a slow, undulating motion that, to my astonishment, felt at that moment wholly natural and appropriate.

Natalia began to calm down. The howling softened into gentle moans, which in turn slowed until they were nothing but the languid in-and-out of her breath. Natalia opened the tissue she had scrunched in her hand and blew her nose, took the clean tissue I held out to her with my other hand, and dried her eyes. Then she rolled onto her back and looked at me.

"Thank you," she whispered. "I'd be eternally grateful if you could turn the painting away. Next time, could we return to the subject of my sexuality? It's easier for me to talk about that. Could you think of a simple exercise for me?"

I removed my hand, stood up from the couch and walked back to my chair. My legs felt weak, but by now the magic had evaporated and I resumed my professional persona. "Well, how about we continue with your experiences of childhood," I suggested, picking up my notebook.

Natalia seemed keen on the idea, and I continued developing the exercise in my familiar manner, intuitively, improvising, as though what happened a moment ago was simply a bad dream. "As we've already dealt with holes, now perhaps we could take a closer look at the extremities, the limbs. How about the supporting words 'arms' and 'legs'? And why not 'head' too—let's include that. Do you think this is something you could work with?"

RECOVERY PROGRAM
WEEK 4

Infantile experiences.
Instruction: Incorporate the supporting words "head," "arms" and "legs."

"As a child, I had a friend—a different friend from the one thrashed with the belt—and one day I asked her, 'If you had to choose, which would you rather be: a head without a body or a body without a head?' She was a smart child and replied, 'I'd be the head, of course.' I couldn't understand it. I thought about her head, imagined placing it on the floor, and there it talked, opening and closing its mouth and rolling its eyes, its neck stuck to the rug. The sight repulsed me. 'Why on earth would you want to be just a head?' I asked, and she replied, 'So I'd still be able to think.' Without a second thought, I knew I would much prefer to be a body. The body has legs, and whereas a head can think by itself, legs can walk by themselves. Where would my friend's head go if it got tired of sitting on the rug? Would it have enough energy to roll over? Looking at my friend's head,

I decided it wouldn't; it would stay propped right there in the middle of the rug until the end of days, unless someone picked it up like a ball and carried it off. I couldn't imagine anybody wanting to so much as touch the head, it was just so horrifying. And if someone did, or if they took such pity on the lonely head that they were able to overcome the inevitable sense of revulsion, the head would always be at the mercy of its bearer. The head might say, 'Take me into the living room, I want to watch TV.' But, out of malice, the bearer might decide to take the head into the kitchen instead—or even worse, the toilet. What would the head do then? It might start making a racket, shouting, bellowing and swearing, but then people might become even more irritated and throw it out the window, and this would be the end of the head, surely a severed head can die from being thrown out of a window just like a person can? I would much rather be just a body. I wouldn't have to worry about thinking. In fact, it would be quite wonderful to be free of thoughts. Didn't my friend consider what she would do once she'd done enough thinking? Maybe she'd fall asleep, I assume heads can sleep, but the following day she would have to wake up again and then the thinking would start again; what else is a head to do? I, on the other hand, would be able to move. I wouldn't be able to see in front of me, because my eyes would be with my head, cut off and thrown away, and which would have ceased to be a part of me. And so I would feel my way forward. Perhaps I'd crawl—I would have a pair of arms, after all. I'd have arms, legs and a torso; think of the possibilities! I could have rubbed myself to orgasm, a practice I started when I was eleven. A mere head can't masturbate, but someone might stick their penis into the mouth of a mere head. Hadn't my friend thought of any of this? A mere head might turn into a frightful vessel for male oral pleasure, because there must undoubtedly be a man in some corner of the world who wouldn't be the least perturbed to grip my friend's hair and thrust his member into her mouth and move it back and forth, faster and faster, all the way to climax. Smart though she was, my friend probably hadn't envisaged a scenario like this. This man—let's call him Gabriel—could have taken my friend's head on vacation with him. In my rampant imagination, bad men always travel a lot. They leave the ugly traces of their bad deeds in a hotel room, for others to clear up, and so continue their journey with a clear conscience. They don't have emotions. They have to stick their tongue into their victims' entrails in order to experience pleasure. This Gabriel of ours might have transported my friend's head in a gym bag like any old piece of equipment, and if my friend had threatened to reveal her kidnapper by screaming, the man might have said, 'Make a sound and I'll throw you over the railings and nobody will be able to save you.' And what might Gabriel have done with me? My headless body would have provided him with at least two orifices that he might conceivably have enjoyed entering. But it would have been much more difficult to handle me than my friend, because unlike her I'd be multidimensional, not round, unlike her I'd be heavy, not light, large, not small, and what's more I'd be able to move independently. Sure, Gabriel might have chained me in a cold, dank basement with a stinking old mattress on the concrete floor so he could have me by force whenever he wished. Even I hadn't imagined this scenario, but now that I think of it I understand that I wouldn't have cared much, being a mere body without a brain and with all possible thoughts left in my severed head, which was no longer mine. So there were many plausible reasons to choose the body instead of the head. In fact, I'd very much like to explain these reasons to my friend, whose answer to that question twenty-eight years ago was, in my opinion, objectively speaking, completely wrong; but speaking to her now would be impossible as we're no longer friends, I don't know where she lives these days, what she does, I don't even know if she's alive."

Natalia arrived for our fourth recovery session with four sheets of paper, each folded into a square. In familiar fashion, she lay down on the couch, placed one of the folded pieces of paper on her stomach and propped the clock on top of the paper. Then she unfolded two pieces of paper and began to read. She didn't stammer while reading and didn't allow her emotions to get the better of her; in fact, she enunciated the words with almost deliberate monotony. Even Gabriel, the patron saint of couriers, postmen and stamp collectors whom Natalia had turned into the terrible rogue of her story, was a seamless part of her steady narration.

After finishing the text, Natalia placed the papers in front of the clock on her chest and waited.

"Thank you," I said, clearing my throat, which felt suddenly extremely dry. "How did this text come about?"

Natalia bent her left knee and hauled herself further up the couch. "Did I do badly, writing such a horrible story?" she asked, her voice slightly anxious.

I noted that Natalia used the word *badly*, that she formulated the question like a small child whose vocabulary and, indeed, understanding might not yet include the idea of doing *wrong*. Of course, even newborn babies have an innate early sense of morality acquired through a process of emotional contagion. For instance, we see this when, upon hearing one hungry baby crying, the entire ward will start to wail en masse. Even rats have the ability to sense the emotional fluctuations of other rats. This is the way Mother Nature intended things, and in this way she loves and cares for each and every little rodent. As long as one mouse sees a fox and takes fright, the whole colony will suddenly be in a state of panic, ready to flee. Nature is wise. It created us as mirrors to each other, because things are good like that. A child, or Natalia regressed to a childlike state, practices coexistence by reacting to other people's emotions and attributing words to them. In this reality, *bad* is the quality of an object, just as the weather may be *bad* or a shoe might fit *badly*. Thus, a child who defines itself as *bad* sees itself through other people's eyes, though it is as innocent as a broken moccasin, as free of responsibility as an autumnal storm. Only when the notion of wrongness penetrates a child's understanding does the child truly begin to appreciate the cause-and-effect implications of its actions.

But no, Natalia hadn't done wrong by writing a story like that.

In this regard, the layering process is akin to classical psychoanalysis. It's not in a therapist's purview to condemn; instead, we ask what things mean. We accept everything our clients produce, as these are the raw tools of healing association.

"It was Saturday morning, I was sitting in the kitchen, a cup of coffee and a sheet of square paper in front of me, thinking about extremities, as you suggested," she continued. "I thought of the head, the arms and legs. I drew an amoeba in the middle of the paper and began brainstorming. You know, the way little children doodle things on paper. This amoeba quickly turned into a spider, and at the end of each of its legs I wrote banal words that came to mind, words like *shoes, mittens, hat, crown, tiara, Alice band, ponytail, hairpin*, and so on. I began to think of girlhood, dressing up as a princess, discovering my mother's makeup bag. I don't remember what it felt like parading in front of my family, though I'm sure I did so. I put the paper away and began washing the dishes, and it was then that the conversation I had with my friend back in the 1980s suddenly sprang to mind."

Natalia began telling me about the friend who was two years older than her and with whom she had practiced the art of reasoning. While with her other friend, the one who was routinely beaten, she generally gallivanted outdoors, with this friend she spent most of the time indoors, and usually in the dark, too, as this girl's bedroom had a large aquarium full of strange and wonderful creatures, angelfish the color of rainbow trout, banjo catfish scurrying near the bottom of the tank and pugnacious tiger barbs, which they watched together while they reasoned together. No adults ever hurt this friend. The girl was allowed to keep to herself and to be as weird as she wanted—and she truly was weird, and this attracted Natalia.

"In fact, weirdness has always fascinated me," said Natalia. "I worry about becoming bored of people. I worry about the disappointment that boring people awaken in me and the guilt that always follows my disappointment. Of course I realize you shouldn't categorize people like this. Boring or interesting, it doesn't matter, everybody has their own place, their own unique human worth. The world would grind to a halt without boring people!"

Natalia uttered these last words in a way that told me she couldn't care less whether the world came to a halt or not. As far as she was concerned, the world might simply hold its breath while she and her oddball friend focused on solving the great philosophical conundrums, like the riddle of whether to be merely a head or merely a body.

"You didn't feel bored in your friend's company," I concluded, ignoring Natalia's attempt at a virtue-signaling smirk. "And you recalled your conversation while you were washing the dishes. What happened then?"

In a traditional therapy session, after a story like this the first thing to which I would have paid particular attention was Natalia's claim that she started pleasuring herself at the age of eleven. As with almost all children, this most probably caused her a deep sense of guilt. Having said that, in a traditional therapy session I never would have heard a story like this. More traditionally, matters tend to arise through the shoes/mittens/hat type of association exercise that Natalia too had tried.

By contrast, our layering process gradually leads the subject into a world of surprising comparisons and contrasts. In this way, the subject's subconscious worldview becomes apparent more quickly and vividly than in any other known treatment method. I compare this process to the intellectual montages one finds in Soviet films, a genre I greatly admire. At its heart, this is an editing technique that reveals to the viewer the deeper significance of a scene within a short stretch of time, visually, without the use of text frames. Naturally, in a therapy setting we must of necessity rely on language—*c'est le malheur de la parole*—and what's more, it goes without saying that the matters under discussion are many times more complicated than, say, the societal power relations in Eisenstein's *Strike*. In a montage of two images, Eisenstein's film compares the extinguishing of the revolution with the slaughter of a bull. In her "extremity" exercise, Natalia compared children's imaginary games with rape, something to which she had already alluded in her text *In the Courtyard at the Ukrainian Embassy*. In this larger image, revealed through intellectual montage, a child's self-gratification is merely a fly in the ointment. Natalia compared sexuality to violence, and we must figure out why.

In layer therapy, it is crucial to address the moment at which the suggestive support words forming the basis of an exercise begin to "seed." With this term, borrowed from the field of botany and whose expressive potency was duly noted at my doctoral defense, I seek to elucidate a guided associative process that, at its best, can produce new subspecies, new deep thoughts. The central contention of my theory is that deep thoughts, which arise from associative "seeding" in the manner of an intellectual montage, feel true throughout the client's body. They represent holistic information that in its own way differs significantly from analytical reflection, which many traditional psychoanalysts hold in great regard. The strongest and most contested point of my research is that, regardless of whether it takes place in the context of therapy, analytical reflection only produces surface thoughts. In turn, surface thoughts foster tautological information, and deeply traumatized people like Natalia are often drawn into their current. They know very well what is wrong with them and what is causing their problems. Often, they are able to put this knowledge into words so skillfully that the more feebleminded therapists are easily taken in by it. Quacks like this are a dime a dozen, they think people like Natalia are "interesting," and with that we are already on the road to perdition as these idiots, rubber-stamped by the Mental Health Supervisory Board, wouldn't recognize countertransference if it slapped them in the face.

I doubt I would be revealing a great secret by telling you that there are, lamentably, a great many members of my profession whose intelligence quotient is not very high and who have about as much sensitivity as a plastic spoon. In their hands, delicate and intelligent people—nearly always women—become even more agonized. Like dry sponges, these poor subjects suck up all the subliminal messages the therapist feeds them, and with that they start producing pulp worthy of Hollywood. From the perspective of their recovery, however, this can be very detrimental because a person seeking out therapy primarily desires to be seen, not admired: *esse est percipi.*

And so I brought Natalia back to the dishwashing situation. Something happened at the moment Natalia's hands were immersed in that hot, soapy water, hidden beneath the suds. She felt the contour of a familiar object in her hands, a red-hot stainless steel knife, perhaps, or a warm porcelain plate, when a distant memory suddenly came to mind. The memory was followed by a deluge of new questions and observations that didn't belong in the mental landscape of Natalia's childhood. This is exactly how my method is supposed to work; it is designed to bounce and rebound.

"I left the dishes and rushed to the computer," Natalia continued. "I thought I'd write a few lines about the difficulties of being merely a head, because it was only when I stood there washing the dishes that I realized why my friend was wrong. In some way I already knew this at the time but couldn't argue my position. Besides, I almost always rescinded my own thoughts whenever my friend started speaking. She was very convincing. Now I felt the need for some payback. I started writing. Before I knew it, three hours had passed, and I just carried on writing. And guess what? I even wrote a letter to you!"

From under the clock, Natalia pulled out the rest of her papers.

"Do you remember our first session, when I told you about a situation that had hurt me? The one I wrote about through my metaphorical story that opened up the symbolism during our session? It's been bugging me since. I've thought about one of your supportive words many times, Doctor. The only noun phrase, *the last man*. You see, there have been many last men in my life. The film critic I told you about is one of them. In the poem I wrote for you, he and another idiot are fused together. The critic represents the centaur's upper body while the other one is just the rear end of a horse. I wanted you to know the whole story. That's why I wrote you a letter."

Natalia waved the paper in my direction, still lying on her back, without looking at me. I leaned over and took it from her. I was about to unfold the piece of paper when Natalia suddenly shouted: "No, please, don't read it now! Read it when I'm not here. If you want to read it, that is. You don't have to. And we don't need to talk about this ever again. I've said what I had to say, with the same energy I put into today's exercise. I'm free at last!"

Natalia's voice didn't convince me; on the contrary, her last words sounded less like a statement and more like a question. Behind the words, her tone was asking me whether her pain had finally been consigned to history. Or would she continue to suffer whenever she thought of the matter, had it all been in vain?

"Thank you for the letter, Natalia. Of course I'll read it," I said in a gentle voice, trying to exude calm though my hands were trembling. I suddenly realized this was the first time a client had written me a private letter. Clients have given me books, records, drawings, small sculptures, all manner of pseudo-artistic scribblings; after all, over the years I have garnered a reputation as a therapist with a particular understanding of artistic clients' problems. But all these gifts were given to me as a show of thanks after our final meeting. The letter, whose contents Natalia did not wish to discuss further, seemed to me a rather odd, portentous gesture, and I wanted to read it at the first opportunity.

Natalia sighed heavily as though I had lifted a great weight from her shoulders. Then she began to thank me, and once she started, she decided to express gratitude for another matter too.

"And thank you, dear doctor, for taking *Ear-Mouth* down from the wall. You have no idea how much the gesture means to me."

In accordance with Natalia's wishes, I had moved *Ear-Mouth* to the floor and propped it behind the Russian blue armchair, facing the wall. The painting was surprisingly heavy, but I promised myself that I would rehang it once Natalia had gone. The frame had left a distinct yellowed mark on the wall and I hadn't the slightest inclination to paint over the plasterwork, let alone to find another work of art to replace my beloved canvas. And so, once a week, I took *Ear-Mouth* down and put it back in place an hour later. I decided to think of this operation in much the same way as the stretching exercises my physiotherapist had suggested, because I believed that one day we would once again look at that painting, that is, the trauma that *Ear-Mouth* represented for Natalia.

As I vividly remembered, a round, blood-red lacquer seal was attached to the back of the painting, and from the center of that small circular seal rose the letters *e.w.* Such a woman was Elise Watteauville: refined and allusive, constrained but self-aware, strong, proud, *sans pareille*. She didn't want to sign the front of her paintings. For her, the painting *was* the signature. In order to make life more difficult for forgers, she had created her very own seal, and the composition of the red coloring used in it was known only to her and a handful of carefully selected experts. Focusing my eyes on those two gleaming graphemes, I began to formulate something as a way of bringing the session to an end.

"No need to thank me. Of course I took it down. It's my job to make this office a safe space for you."

The ticking hands of Natalia's clock showed about two minutes to two, so I knew she wouldn't voluntarily speak another word. I continued regardless, as I wanted to tell her the subject of our next session before the alarm started clanging. "We could move to the world of adulthood, for a change. How about next time you tell me about an experience that was particularly significant to you? Several, if you prefer."

Natalia mumbled—that was all she was prepared to concede to the final minutes of our session. She had decided she would not allow her voice to be cut off by the clamor of the clock, though it was she who had brought the old contraption here and set the alarm in the first place.

"My only instruction is that you build your account around an item of your choosing," I continued. "It can be any item, concrete or symbolic, allegorical or even mythical—why not? As long as it is linked to the experience you choose to tell me about. Do you get the idea?"

Amid the silence, which I took as a yes, we sat together waiting for the clock to ring.

MY DEAREST DOCTOR!

I shall begin by citing a poem that you, as one who appreci-
ates art, will recognize in an instant:

> *I turned that woman, held her close,*
> *But, friends, would you ever suppose,*
> *That she didn't have one of those?*

Let this serve as an introduction to my little letter, in which I
will try once again to explain everything I was trying to put
behind me in our first pain-displacement exercise. This too is
a story about separation. As soon as that relationship ended
I started ranting, saying this would be THE LAST MAN I let
into my life, though around the corner the next last man was
about to walk right into my arms.

Nonetheless, I always learned something from these
encounters. Such as that hell is full of men whose wives have
mysteriously lost one or more of their body parts. Did you
know this? Do you see people lying on your couch, wives who
have woken up to realize they are missing this or that or that

or that? I doubt it very much! What about their angry, desperate or indifferent husbands—do they lie on the same couch as me? Do they tell you, the way I'm telling you now, how they have spent years fumbling in the darkness beneath the blankets for this and this and this and this, and how one beautiful day they decided to stop trying altogether, because life can be fine just the way it is, and allowed themselves to experience freedom? I doubt it.

Be that as it may, they certainly lie in my bed. They sprawl so languidly, so freely, that I have to snap at them for the sake of balance. I retreat into myself, to a place where I can mope in peace, without anybody seeing, because their freedom is not my freedom, and it's started eating away at me.

It was after one particular copulation that I finally realized this matter in all its horrific brightness. Suddenly, *post coitum*, I was incredibly angry. But I was so stupid-stupid-stupid-stupid-stupid-stupid-stupid that I couldn't understand why I felt like pressing a pillow against the damned loser's face when he started kissing me, whispering that life was just one long party, one big JAM sandwich (his visits generally coincided with my period), one or, more likely, two bottles of pre-chilled Blanc de Blancs Brut in the fridge, one big rapturous, drink-fueled buzz. That's what life with me is like. But what about his own life?

I wanted to see how this man who had granted himself freedom really lived. And what his wife was like, the mother of his three adorable children, who, if his stories were to be believed, had in some extraordinary way lost not only her genitals but her ability to speak and even her legs, at least that's how I understood it. Naturally, this man didn't want me for *only that*. He wanted everything, friendship *and* a pussy. Making love *and* walks in the countryside. Long phone calls *and* quick lunchtime hanky-panky.

At this point, someone wiser than me might have said: "He's just cherry-picking. Run away, Natalia, while you still can!" But nobody was there to give me advice. I didn't run away. I empathized with him, so much so that between my legs I almost grew a throbbing penis, sore from lack of action. I empathized so much that I began to believe the right to sex must be enshrined in the United Nations' Universal Declaration of Human Rights. Why shouldn't I do my bit, however small? Why shouldn't I help a man tormented by abstinence, and in doing so help myself too?

The man had done everything he could, or so he told me, to be both a friend and a lover to his wife. He'd hired a babysitter, vacuumed the rugs, he bought her a box of chocolates, booked a surprise trip abroad. But at the crucial moment, time and again his beloved wife turned her back on him and barricaded herself behind their children, he told me and stuck a finger inside me.

One night, after we'd been frolicking around for a while, sleeping off and on, I got out of bed. I was both hungry and furious. Our little SECRET had exhausted me, it didn't feel like the almond hidden in the Christmas porridge anymore, the sugar or the cinnamon, because I was a prisoner in my very own HOME, locked in endless waiting, in an eternal state of readiness, and I finally began to understand.

I decided to call a spade a spade.

I went into the kitchen, prepared a meal. I woke the man, sat him down at the table. We spoke about this and that. I don't care to remember what meaningless topics we covered to bore one another after a month's break. I do remember that he spoke more than I did. He ate and spoke as though he was eating and speaking in his own HOME. I ran my fork through the avocado salad I had gathered around the scallops on my plate and waited for the right moment.

We were halfway through the bottle of wine when I finally did it.

I said: "You come and go, you schedule me in your calendar along with your business trips. I don't like this anymore. No matter how I look at it, I feel used. And there's another problem too, your wife, who as you've told me turns her back on you, as if to say, 'Please take care of your sexual needs somewhere else.' How do I know if that's true, if you don't even know it yourself? What do you actually know about your wife?"

I didn't really want to know what he did or didn't know about his wife, so I continued without letting him speak.

"Exactly, it's all about *your* sexual needs. *Your* human rights, which I help you fulfill. Did you know my life stops when the clock reaches eight in the evening, the time you've told me you're going to show up, though you're never even remotely punctual? I wait, and as I wait I become nervous, and when I'm nervous I stop living, stop being myself, my HOME stops being my HOME, it turns into a damn waiting room. This has to stop. I can't do it anymore."

The man didn't understand in the slightest. He made stupid faces at me. He took my half-full wineglass, filled it to the brim, and reminded me—as if I could have forgotten—that we met not just in my HOME but in other places too, like Äkäskero, western Lapland, Madrid, the Maldives. He also found it necessary to remind me that I had agreed to our little arrangement, that I was his partner in crime and didn't have the right to moralize about it.

"Don't be so BLACK-AND-WHITE, my little bunny," he cajoled. "It's a win-win situation," he extolled, and without asking permission gave my glass a clink most bold. "Bottoms up!"

I held back a SCREAM and thought of my dear father, who was a thousand times better than this scumbag, and I knew he would have died of shame if he'd seen me with such a Neanderthal. I thought of my father, who, if he had been in my position, wouldn't have hesitated to throw that asshole out of my HOME, which I should have done too, of course, but for better or worse, I am what I am: I started drinking straight from the bottle.

We went back to bed. I allowed him to enter me, though it hurt, though in his hands I was quickly becoming a woman who didn't have "one of those"—which, were it really true, would have been a great deal of use to me, given my current predicament.

In the morning I pretended to be asleep. I let him slip out the door and made myself PROMISE that I'd take care of my dirty laundry in a way that decent women would in my shoes.

That morning I decided to start a new life.

I decided to make a cathartic visit to the man's HOME.

The following Saturday I hopped on a commuter train and traveled fifty kilometers east. I walked another five kilometers through subzero temperatures following the directions on my phone's GPS. *Walk one kilometer, then turn left*, and so I turned, *walk five hundred meters, then turn right*, and so I turned, though many times I almost turned back, and so on until I arrived in front of a white-brick detached house.

The snow had been plowed with geometrical precision. Had that repulsive man asked his wife to sweep the pathways with a broom, and tidy the edges of the snowdrifts with a dustpan and brush? I know snow, and believe me, that snow didn't look plowed; it looked swept. And I know that man, too; I could imagine him with a plow but not with a broom.

I walked up to the porch and rang the doorbell.

The door was opened by a beautiful, dark-haired woman in a fitted, BLUE-AND-RED wraparound dress, its neckline particularly, shall we say, generous. The woman was slender, her chest flat and sinewy. Around her neck she sported a necklace made of small, TRANSPARENT glass beads, and I instantly recognized it as a gift from the man's trip to New York. The woman's husband had brought me a piece of Murano glass jewelry by the Sent sisters on the same business trip—not a glass bead necklace, however, but glass bead earrings that were, as I later established, sixty-five dollars cheaper than the necklace and, what's more, completely useless to me as there are no HOLES in my earlobes, something the idiot hadn't noticed while he was screwing me.

At that moment, I would have given anything to conjure up HOLES in my ears and to slide those glass bead earrings into those HOLES.

"Hello," I said to the woman standing in the doorway, in as calm a voice as I could muster. "I've come to tell you your husband is banging me."

I hadn't thought about what might happen next. I wanted to reveal the betrayal, and myself, then I would trudge back to the station, get on the first train HOME and finally grow up.

The woman looked at me unflinchingly. "Mikael," she shouted without turning her head. "Would you come to the door, please?"

The man, who only five nights ago had stayed the night at

my apartment, appeared next to his wife and placed a hand on her shoulder, that hand whose two fingers he'd stuck up my vagina at least a thousand times.

"Mikael, this woman claims to be having some sort of relation with you."

"It's not true," he said to his wife, and looked at me calmly. "She works for a PR company we deal with. She's responsible for visualizing our communications strategy. She has very serious mental health issues."

"This isn't true," I replied with exaggerated calm, as though I was talking on behalf of another woman altogether. "I met your husband two years ago at a franchise meeting. He's been banging me regularly ever since."

After this, the following dialogue played out:

"This woman is lying."

"Your husband is lying."

"This woman is deeply disturbed."

"Your husband is cheating on you."

"This woman is obsessed. I'm not the only one in our company she's done this to."

"Your husband bought me some Sent sisters jewelry too, when he was in New York on business two months ago."

"Bettina, dearest, she's a stalker. I've reported her to the police."

The man's voice was soft and velvety. He didn't take his eyes off me for a second. He pulled his wife closer and then, all at once, a curious, skewed smile spread across the woman's expressionless face, almost a squint.

"Get yourself a good therapist," she said to me. "You're going to need one."

And with that they closed the door in my face.

The one thing I have learned from this episode is the value of honesty.

After going through a string of terrible therapists and one spell in hospital, I came to your office to learn that noble art.

FEBRUARY 9TH, 2018

Your friend, Natalia

Natalia arrived for our fifth session with a small recording device. "I have an idea," she giggled. "Let's record the lot, *vittu!*"

This was the first but not the last time that Natalia used this vulgar word with the mere intention of swearing. I'm not unfamiliar with curse words, though personally I prefer lighter, more sophisticated swearing, but to my mind, uttered in this way the word simply didn't suit Natalia. To coin a phrase, it just wasn't her style.

Was she trying to imply something else with this choice of word? Perhaps it had something to do with the letter, which for one reason or another she had signed as my "friend." Though seemingly innocuous, that possessive pronoun made the associated noun sound oddly brazen, because it implied something about me in a way that the other phrases Natalia used regularly, "dearest doctor" or "my dear doctor," did not.

Besides, this was the first time she had demonstrably lied to me. At the end of her letter she mentioned having undergone hospital treatment, a matter I could easily verify. It was exactly as I had expected: Natalia hadn't spent a single day in any psychiatric ward.

It couldn't be mere coincidence that after telling this flagrant falsehood, virtually in the same breath, she claims she came to me to learn the "noble art" of honesty. Natalia was testing me, and she had come out with all guns blazing. She had thrown me a conundrum, and as a key to unlocking it she now offered the word *vittu*.

An examination of the situations in which she used this word only further strengthened my hypothesis. Natalia used this vulgar word for "vagina" when she wanted something she thought I might refuse, as if the very utterance of the word *vittu* might blur my judgment and make me more amenable to other suggestions, though in reality the word jarred my ear, making me forget the question in hand altogether.

Still, I had to admit that Natalia was intuitively on the right track; while it denotes the genitals of a woman who has given birth and derives from the Old Swedish *fitta*, meaning "swamp," in the Finnish folkloric tradition the word also historically refers to the gateway separating the earthly world from the underworld, the threshold that the shamans must cross in order to negotiate with the spirit world.

To digress slightly, the Finnish language is not especially

resourceful in this regard. We must look to the treasure troves of Swedish or Old Norse, Russian or some other major language in order to make all the meanings of our own words shine clearly. Things are different in French, for instance, a language that can subtly play with its own words and derivations. I recently read an essay by Jean-Claude Arquette in which the writer observes that the word *la confession* carries with it, almost imperceptibly, the vulgar designation for the female genitals, *le con*. Rather surprisingly, it turns out that the French *vittu* is masculine, but when associated with the idea of confession, it becomes feminine. In his essay, Arquette hazards that only the sacrament of repentance can restore the woman's vagina to its rightful state, redeeming it from the realm of masculine speech. I cannot speak to the truth or otherwise of this provocative statement, but I will say that it would be impossible to express such nuances in Finnish. The only approximation I can think of is *vittunnustus*, a "cunfession" if you will, though this isn't really a word so much as a morphological monstrosity with which it is virtually impossible to create even a single pun.

Natalia quickly took off her coat, shoes, scarf and gloves as she breathlessly explained her fear that our conversations had disappeared "into thin air." Though we had already amassed a considerable amount of written material, there had been even more talking. And where was it all now? Nowhere!

Until now Natalia had never spoken before our sessions officially started. Therapy sessions usually start with the client getting comfortable on the couch, but Natalia was too agitated for this. She paced back and forth across the rug, running her fingers through her hair. Eventually she reached her hand out to shake mine, sat down on the couch, placed the clock in her lap and her handbag next to her. Still she wouldn't lie down properly.

"I realized we have a problem when I started writing you that letter," she continued; I was taken aback that she would refer to a subject she had already told me she was reluctant to discuss any further. "I assume you noticed that I used the supporting words you gave me? I've been thinking about everything you said to me at our first meeting. And I couldn't remember anything. If we'd had the sense to record all our sessions, we would already have reams of material. Imagine!"

Now I was even more skeptical about Natalia's intentions. No matter how hard I tried, I couldn't fathom what the strange elements at the end of the letter, the bizarre arrival at our therapy session, and this latest whimsical request had to do with one another.

Besides, except for research purposes, recorded data is not a constituent part of the layer-therapy method. Naturally I always take notes—paper and pen are the age-old tools of every therapist, just as an Allen wrench and a Phillips screwdriver are indispensable tools for any carpenter. Ultimately, all other technology is subordinate to the truth contained in the notebook. And if I do say so myself, over the years I have become quite the master of note-taking. I find it easy to listen to my client while teasing out the most salient points, the details and digressions amid the tangle of speech. It's part of the professional skill set that this line of work has drummed into me.

"Welcome to our fifth session, Natalia," I began, completely disregarding the fact that she still hadn't lain down on the couch. "Today we're going to discuss your most powerful experiences of adulthood. Would you like to start by telling me about this idea of recording our sessions?"

Natalia swung her legs back and forth and began to explain.

"I doubt it will surprise you to hear that I go to a lot of trouble to prepare for these sessions. And, let me stress, that isn't a problem at all. On the contrary, for the first time in ages I feel like I'm alive! The weeks are no longer crushingly similar, the days meaningless, the nights agonized. You see, things are moving forward."

She tucked a loose curl of hair behind her ear and lowered her voice. The transition was like moving from soft, easily swallowed brioche to bloody beef, a more complicated affair, if we are to view her performance in terms of this classic hamburger metaphor.

"I've written a little poem and a few longer texts. I have drawn a penis. I even wrote you a letter, and it's a good thing I did; sometimes I can't bring myself to talk about the daily grind, all that dick-smelling shit. When I'm home working on these exercises, I am happy, and when I come to your office, I feel content. But each time our session ends, I feel a huge sense of disappointment. I've racked my brains to figure out where it might come from, this disappointment, and I think I've come up with an answer."

Natalia held a dramatic pause and looked up at me. "The things I say, and in particular the way I say them, all disappear without a trace. The same goes for your comments. Our conversations no longer exist."

At that moment one possible and frankly terrifying explanation for Natalia's exclamation of "Let's record the lot, *vittu*" urgently pressed itself into my mind. Had she turned up at my office with a recording device to try to frame me for malpractice? There are rumors throughout our profession of a certain personality type whose only reason for undertaking therapy is to create a public scandal. Until now, I'd considered this nothing more than an urban legend.

I remembered painfully well how only a few weeks ago I'd sat down next to Natalia as she wept—something it goes without saying I should never have done—and how I had gently touched her. And sung to her. I might as well admit that after this episode I seriously considered closing my practice completely and taking early retirement, but my dear mentor eventually brought me to my senses. My mentor advised me to be careful with Natalia, but reminded me that in her I finally had the kind of client I'd dreamed of finding while writing my PhD. It's no wonder I'd become overenthusiastic. Nonetheless, in future I would simply have to channel this enthusiasm more delicately.

I kept a straight face and explained to Natalia that in layer therapy, just as in any form of psychotherapy, a free-flowing dialogue is of the utmost importance. The idea is to foster the confidential exchange of words within the confines of the therapist's professional ethics, an exchange hindered neither by moralism nor etiquette, neither perfectionism nor performance anxiety, and that the only restriction, critically important for the client's return to health, is that of time: the forty-five minutes of paid time that create the safe parameters for each session.

"You're worried about this material disappearing," I continued, as I wanted to bring discussion of the tape recorder to a close as swiftly as possible. "You realize I take notes throughout our sessions?"

Of course she knew this. She'd seen my notepad—I don't try to hide it from my clients in any way—and heard my pen scratching across the paper behind her head. But it seemed my notes weren't enough for her.

"Everybody has reams of notes," she scoffed, pulling from her bag a plastic envelope containing a thick pile of squared papers. "I have enough scribbled notes to fill a room. These are the ones I used to write down my thoughts on pornography. Do you remember? The stories about holes that I produced a few weeks ago? This is another of my problems: I can't bring myself to destroy these papers, but I don't know what to do with them either."

Natalia shook the plastic envelope in the air. "Can I give these to you? You can return to them and work on them, if you wish—after all, you were present in these sessions too," she said, as though the presence of a therapist at a therapy session were simply a fortunate coincidence.

I took Natalia's envelope, bewildered. We had never talked about what happens to the written material related to her exercises. In my PhD, I assert that from a therapy perspective texts produced by the client are only of peripheral importance, as everything essential takes place right there on the couch. Until now, all my clients have kept this written material to themselves, representing as they do a private space akin to that of a diary.

I realized I would have to latch onto Natalia's last sentence as soon as our session officially began. Right as Natalia lay down properly on the couch, I would have to say: "Of course I can look after your notes. But I'm interested to hear how you think I should work with them."

I didn't have time to develop this thought any further when I saw Natalia reach for her bag again. This time she pulled out a mini-cassette recorder, which reminded me of my ancient Nokia 2110 cell phone, said "*ta-daa!*," by my count for the third time in my presence, and handed me the device. Then she lowered her bag to the floor, positioned herself on the couch in exaggerated slow motion, almost ceremonially, and placed the alarm clock on her stomach.

I'm well acquainted with recording devices; after all, I'd recorded hundreds of hours of material for my PhD. Transliterating that material—not to mention analyzing it—occupied me for the best part of several years. However, the recorder I used was digital, whereas Natalia's contraption was almost an antique. I was sure the magnetic tapes would crackle as they turned, not loudly, but just enough.

"Let's begin, shall we?" I said, and carefully placed the recorder on the small table next to me. "So, you want to record our sessions. Would you like to tell me what you plan to do with these recordings?"

Natalia was silent. Maybe she was searching for the right words, maybe wondering whether there was a hint of disparagement in my voice. Or—the thought suddenly occurred to me— was she waiting for me to press the Record button? Did she want me to start the recording now?

I felt my strength vanishing, felt as though I was draining into the almond-green armchair like a viscous liquid, not seeping through the upholstery but remaining on the surface of the fabric in a heap of jelly. Is this what Natalia had meant with her victorious cry of "Let's record the lot, *vittu*"? Recording absolutely everything, recording the conversation about whether or not to record things? Stubborn silence whenever the Stop or Pause buttons were on?

Thank goodness this wasn't the case, but I will say that if Natalia had chosen to remain utterly silent until she heard my finger press the REC button, we would have been in trouble. I cannot and will not be blackmailed, explicitly or otherwise. Treatment procedures occur within a set of mutually agreed parameters. Under no circumstances could I switch on the recorder without first having a thorough conversation about the matter. Not even for Natalia.

My relief was immeasurable when Natalia finally opened her mouth. "Yes, I would like our future sessions to be recorded." After a short hesitation, she added coyly: "If that's all right with you, Doctor."

And so began our negotiation, which I will describe in terms of a tennis match, the classic model of argument and counterargument. It was Natalia who served first: "I don't consider myself a special case, I need you to know that. And that's exactly why I'm convinced that someone, somewhere, is suffering just like me. It might be someone who lives long after I'm gone, when I haven't existed for decades, centuries even! Still, I want to be able to say to that person, whoever it may be, 'You're not alone, my sister, my brother.' Do you understand? If the struggle is simply for myself, then all this feels pretty damn pointless."

I must admit I didn't quite follow Natalia's train of thought. It's perfectly normal for people to undergo therapy for themselves. Each of us has the right to our own well-being. Besides, I think every individual is worthy of a song, or maybe they are the song itself, an entire song cycle, Schubert's *Winterreise*. Is there a more beautiful thing in this world than the full realization of our potential? The human spirit blossoming, freed from all shackles?

I didn't try to convince Natalia just how unique and valuable she was, but instead hurried to return the ball to her side of the court. I was actually quietly pleased that the conversation had moved in this direction, that is to say, to Natalia herself. We needed to stay focused on her. I struck the ball hard, the power of the blow taking even me by surprise. "So you want to make your suffering public? Perhaps you're planning to write a book on the subject?"

Natalia seemed unperturbed and returned the ball to me, this time with spin. "No, not me. A professional person. You, perhaps! And only if you think the subject warrants a more public discussion. I have no desire to be thrust into the spotlight. I'm a private person. When I started feeling unwell, I just hoped that somewhere I might find a story about a woman like me, the kind of story I might read and realize I'm not alone in this world."

I duly noted that Natalia didn't specify what she meant by "a woman like me." A woman who thinks about sex all the time?

I quickly improvised my next move, as I too belong, or at least I want to belong, to the *carpe diem* school of thought. I wanted Natalia to explain what kind of book she thought was missing from the world.

"I assume you've read everything relating to female sexuality from cover to cover," I began in a voice of studied, heightened neutrality. "You've read *Madame Bovary, Story of O, Venus in Furs*?" To my mind this was—and remains—a perfectly matter-of-fact question. The seed of a new exercise tingled in my mind: Natalia should rewrite the plot of a classic novel using her own experiences.

This ball, which I thought I'd struck gently but firmly, went straight into the net. Natalia raised her shoulders and turned toward me, a look of disgust on her face. Then she lay down again and puffed, violently blowing the air from between her lips, almost in lieu of spitting, as though the act of moving, turning and glaring at me hadn't already expressed enough disdain.

This was the first time I felt shame in Natalia's presence. Immediately afterward I was ashamed of that shame. I wished I'd phrased the question differently, then instantly berated myself for wishing such a thing. One professional hazard in the psychotherapy community is the acute sense of self-awareness one acquires, and it is something that alas we cannot even switch off in the company of our friends, let alone our clients.

In a matter of seconds, I had driven myself off the court. I'd become mired in a sinking swamp of regret. I knew this place, of course; I know all such dark and stinking recesses of the mind, but I don't feel the need to wallow in negative thoughts. And so I began laying a boardwalk to help me cross the bog. I asked myself—not Natalia—what I had said wrong. Had I chosen the wrong examples? Was my client's reaction a form of projection? Willfulness masked as arrogance? And why had it happened right then? Why did those books trigger such a reaction? It's not as if the titles I'd mentioned were in any way substandard. If I had been talking about trashy novels, romance novels full of verbal detritus, then I would have understood Natalia's consternation. But I had plucked these examples from the canon, so surely that couldn't have been the problem. Besides, Natalia had eagerly latched onto the volume of poetry, which I'd given her along with many other titles, before stuffing it full of knuckledusters and fisting. What was bothering her now? Did she hold poetry in higher regard than prose?

Natalia interrupted my self-reflection. She wrenched me back to *terra firma*, picked up the ball lying by the net and struck it confidently. "I want to have faith in my recovery," she assured me, avoiding the question. There was no longer any trace of disdain in her voice. "And I believe in your methods, Doctor. I'm enjoying this! And if you like something, then it can't be wrong. Isn't that right?"

Without waiting for a response, she gave me a suggestion.

"Assuming I recover, assuming there's room in my life for more than just these exhausting sexual fantasies, it would be good to tell other people how my recovery happened. I mean, in this world you can never have too much of a support network. Shall we make an initial deal?"

Our negotiations were reaching their conclusion.

"I cannot guarantee you a book, Natalia," I said after a moment's consideration. "But for my part we may record the material for posterity. I have only one condition: I don't want to use an analog recorder, because it hisses when it's switched on. I have a high-quality digital recorder, which is silent and won't disturb our conversation. Is that acceptable to you?"

"Yes!" Natalia whooped with relief.

"One more thing, Doctor," she continued, her voice suddenly thin, almost fearful. "At home I started thinking about today's exercise, my experiences of adulthood. It was so easy it was almost frightening. My mind was flooded with images, which were real, and thoughts, which were real too. I wanted to talk about them straightaway. But who could I have told? Who would have listened to me? You see, I couldn't wait for Tuesday to come!"

Natalia mustered her courage and finally spat out what it was she had to say. "So I went out and bought this recorder. And I did something I shouldn't have done. I recorded the exercise at home in advance."

By now Natalia's voice was taut with excitement. The last sentence was so tense that her voice yodeled like a young boy's and came out in a strangled, almost earsplitting wail.

The tension, which I now realized had made my shoulders rock-solid, finally abated. I sighed with relief. So this is why Natalia had brought the tape recorder to our session, this is what her rambunctious *vittu* really meant. I asked a question in order to fill the silence, though by now the answer was perfectly obvious to me. "And the recording you made at home is inside the recorder?"

Yes, there it was, wound back to the beginning of the tape. One story followed by two bonus stories, three memories in total. Natalia had made each of these accounts more complete by using an object of her choosing.

"My humble wish," she whispered, "is that we could listen to the first tape now and the next two at our next sessions. Would that be at all possible?"

I picked up the recorder from the table and ran my fingers across the black buttons. When my forefinger identified the embossed triangle, I pressed Play.

RECOVERY PROGRAM
WEEKS 5-6-7

Unforgettable experiences from adult life.
Instruction: In this exercise incorporate
a device that best characterizes the experience.
Do with it whatever you wish.

MR. DIAGONAL TESTICLE & THE HERMENEUTICS

One of my lovers had a diagonal testicle. He had been suffering from birth from a condition called cryptorchidism, in other words his left testicle hadn't dropped into the scrotum but had remained hidden inside the pelvic cavity and therefore hung at a distinct diagonal angle in relation to the right testicle, which was where it was supposed to be. The man was a urologist by profession. In other words, he had made an entire profession out of his suffering; that's what all people do when they suffer in such a way that Shame is omnipresent. I studied art history because I understood at an early age that whenever we create an image, be it an oil painting, a watercolor, an ink-jet printout, a chromatogenous photograph, a drawing in pastel, sepia, pencil or asphalt lacquer, and when that image is on a defined surface, a board, and whatever the base material of that work, jute canvas, acrylic board, corrugated iron, PVC fabric, a glass-blown mirror, Japanese wax paper, transparent paper, then it exists, with a single glance you can take it in and commit it to memory, and you can always return to it and look at it again, though after the fall of 1995 I was unable to look at *Ear-Mouth* again. Indeed, as early as high school I realized that Things, the kind of things that deserved a capital letter, like Shame, which I have tried to make my dearest friend, should be framed—and not only framed but displayed for all to see, for us to confront on a daily basis. Framing Things strips them of the squalor of secrecy. And so I studied art history and even harbored dreams of becoming an artist myself, though I quickly understood while sitting in lecture halls looking at slides of Rembrandts, Giorgiones, Michelangelos, Tizianos, Dürers and Botticellis that I didn't have the skill, that my meager gifts would never rise as high as they should even if I were to shut myself away in an isolated cabin in no-man's-land and paint for sixteen years. I realized I'd be better off reading and looking, honing my eye and my intellect, and leaving my hands to other kinds of work, to the work of love. And so I masturbated this urologist, I masturbated him with great gusto, saving neither effort nor energy. Because in addition to having a diagonal testicle of which he was ashamed, he had great difficulty penetrating a woman like me. His member was rather large *an sich*, it was perky, sinewy and veiny, right up until he tried to move it closer to my vagina, but as soon as the tip of his penis touched an intimate part of me, it became small, miserable, shriveled, soft and useless. He imagined that there existed within me a *vagina dentata*, and his member became flaccid. Every single time. Why on earth hadn't he studied gynecology instead? Instead of using his studies to nurse his diagonal testicle and his penis, which was always limp in the presence of women, he should have acquainted himself with the female anatomy. By examining thousands upon thousands of pussies, he could have gathered empirical experience to reassure himself that there was nothing inside a woman that could harm his member. Of course, a vagina can cramp and the man's penis can momentarily become caught inside the snatch, and for the man it can feel as though that snatch might suck his tool right into its depths. But there isn't a single snatch in the history of the world that has crushed a man's penis so much as to render it useless, and not a single penis in the world has disappeared into the dark recesses of any snatch. A cramping vagina will eventually spit the penis out and eject a long trail of mucus too, and for a moment or two the man's tool might be sensitive to the touch, raw, though only in a figurative sense. A few hours later, or at the very latest after a good night's sleep, it will be ready for action again. My urologist was a clever man and he understood all this, but his penis was stupid and didn't understand anything. That's why I used my hand with him, so much so that I almost gave myself repetitive strain injury. I was consciously pushing aside the Shame that his Shame had caused within me, and I yanked and yanked. *It's the only humane thing to do*, I repeated to myself, *so, so humane*, and I yanked and yanked some more. You appreciate, dear doctor, that I simply had to masturbate him? I enjoy it very much, but until now I'd always thought this was a simple matter of foreplay, the overture to a very well-known series of events, a warm-up that would inevitably lead to his entering me and sooner or later ejaculating inside me. Now I was forced to learn that my innermost space in this short-lived love affair was in fact my lubricated hand, which, unlike my mouth and my pussy, didn't have teeth. We were reciprocal, giving each other love alternately. And allow me to add, so that the situation doesn't appear too simple, that this love involved a searing misery that over time became a vital part of our private enjoyment. My urologist often wept. He succumbed to the sorrow that his inability to penetrate me caused him. He sobbed into my hair and ejaculated in my hand. He taught me new facets of Shame, such as that it is possible to drown Shame with tears. He told me that Shame was a product of the late Silurian period, a fossilized millipede with millions of synonymous sisters, all of which were born at the same time. They pushed their way out of the *Ur*-pussy, the *Ur*-anus, the *Ur*-urethra, the *Ur*-nostril and the *Ur*-mouth, like us and our *Ur*-excrement, our *Ur*-urine, our *Ur*-blood and *Ur*-mucus. My urologist was also interested in German hermeneutics, which he had once chosen as a minor subject to support his diagonal testicle. Very soon I too learned to appreciate that the magic prefix *Ur*- could be attached to any word at all, and after that there was no need for explanations. Do you see, my dearest doctor? We are finally getting to the Point! *Das Ding-Dong an sich!* I couldn't take my urologist's fascination for hermeneutics particularly seriously. You see, my urologist was a lecturer by nature. Talking aroused him. He delved into his thoughts and stopped looking me in the eye; that was the most unpleasant thing about him. But I tolerated his ramblings because he was good with his tongue. I imagined that since I managed to listen to his stories so patiently, he would feel compelled to lick me until I came. And lick me he did. Our sex wasn't unique, far from it, but it was very instructive. What's more, my urologist helped me view my own genitals in a new way. For the first time I began to understand the power of my snatch. It almost frightened me. What trivial words had been written about the woman's nether regions, and how wrong the men of *belles lettres* were! If they'd listened to my urologist, they would have learned similes far more exciting than their worn-out peaches and apricots. It isn't porcelain waiting behind the panty hose, neither flower beds nor pussy willows nor blue oysters. Waiting down there is a cruel vengeance, a mitt turned inside out, a sweaty killer. The *Ur*-pussy that it's impossible to screw. The boy cried wolf too many times, so within its hairy folds it grew a set of razor-sharp teeth. Despite its dim-wittedness, my urologist's penis was the best raconteur of horror stories in the world. And I was a suitable listener. In light of my previous experiences, I was used to thinking that my pussy was a piece of cake and that the specific kind of cake depended on the eater. To one it was Grandma's Dry Crumb Cake, to another a moist raw cake to be savored and enjoyed, to another a traditional Victoria sponge oozing with strawberry jam, something easy to whet the appetite. I'd never thought of my womanhood as a trap, but now I began to see that possibility too. So I took full advantage of my urologist's pussyphobia and dried up until I was dutifully moistened again. This was another example of our reciprocity. And I must add, so there's no misunderstanding, that despite all our difficulties and the excessive, exhausting hermeneutics, I had a great deal of respect for my lover and his diagonal testicle. As a teenager he had decided not to obey the commandments of Shame, which is admirable. He didn't pull the Lappish knife from his father's sheath and slash to a pulp his pelvic cavity and the testicle hiding inside there, though this is exactly what Shame was commanding him to do. He studied urology, tamed his Shame and opened an office on my street. That's where we first met—on the street, by chance—and for a while we became lovers. My hand made love to his penis, which generously ejaculated over my sheets, leaving them sticky. My ears listened to a lecture on Gadamer as my brain prepared itself for orgasm. My labia made love to his tongue, my whole body tingled with sweat. This love lasted for four months. The relationship ended painlessly when he moved his practice to the other side of town.

[10 MINUTES 57 SECONDS]

MADAME TERRY-TOWEL & THE TENDER BUTTONS

After my weepy urologist I needed a change, something totally different, and boy did I get what I was looking for. It was like a punch in the gut. After the urologist I yearned for a sensitive, listening touch, which I'll try to tell you about now, my dearest doctor—in a voice that isn't my own. You see, I'm scared to death that you'll get bored of this story unless, like me, you're practiced in the art of the tantric lifestyle. If I wasn't so terrible at impersonating people, I'd start imitating the speech of the guru Tirumalai Sivananda, but I can't pull it off. I've decided to make up a voice from my own imagination, and I hope from the bottom of my heart that you don't fall asleep while listening to it. Here we go.

This is the story of Madame Terry-Towel, a woman I met five years ago. She'd been on a long spiritual journey before finally learning to love softness. *Nooo!* Softness is the wrong word! But I can't think of a better one, so I'll use that, k? You'll understand soon. So, five years ago, I was at a crossroads, stuck sitting in a room with big windows looking out in two different directions, but there was no door. *Do you see?* I was all alone, watching my life fly by. I was getting out of another shitty relationship and I thought I was having a breakdown, when suddenly this chick walked into my life, a totally amazing human. She was, like, spiritual and physical all at the same time. But hey, lemme give you some background so you can see where I'm coming from. This girl used to be totally into the BDSM scene, but she told me she'd gotten involved with it for all the wrong reasons. She had a history of abuse, and you know, it's such a fucking cliché that we both started laughing when we talked about it. Like, just 'cause you're into BDSM doesn't mean someone must've diddled you when you were a kid, right? But when she was about thirteen there was this uncle, and he wasn't really right in the head, and yada yada. And so she decided that dealing with the pain in strictly defined circumstances might make the pain go away. Who knew, huh? She decided to let herself go, and she turned into like this total pain slut. She was really into her leather riding crop with added horsehair; even an experienced dom would find it impossible to control the movement of the hairs a hundred percent. She wanted all the really hard-core stuff, some scratches and preferably a little blood too; suede gloves, gentle spanking and all that vanilla stuff was totally not her scene. I was listening to her talking, and I was like, okay, I was totally clueless about this stuff. But this chick didn't have a bad word to say about her BDSM buddies. She only ever met up with sweet little "darklings," as she called them. Lots of them were somewhere on the spectrum, you know. Like, once the rules are strictly defined, it helps them have sex, 'cause they don't have to second-guess everything all the time. Then there's the fact that you can go to these sessions as yourself, with all your imperfections, all your quirks and desires, however wacky, right? But that was her problem. She didn't go as herself. She turned up with her disturbed thirteen-year-old soul rolled up in her arms, then hid it from everyone. As if she'd turned up at the gynecologist with like a fake twat or shat out a plastic shit from the practical-joke store. Then she shut down, though everything went according to the rules, and nobody was allowed to do anything to her except what they'd agreed in advance. So, she tried to off herself. She really tried, and it was only some passerby that saved her. At this point I was, like, wow, 'cause I'd thought of doing myself in loads of times, but I only ever *thought* about it. I mean, I'd think about rope, tall buildings, highways, trains, but I'd always chicken out. I guess there's a pretty big leap—ha, get it?—between thinking about it and actually doing it; I asked if it was like that for her, but she told me she never felt that way, she'd just come up with an idea and go through with it as, like, a spur-of-the-moment decision. I guess she was feeling real bad. And I didn't really get it; how can you decide to die, then, like, only nearly die, without all those infamous second thoughts popping into your head? Anyways, the possibility of dying had totally freaked her out. And that became the line in the sand. And so this chick started actively taking control of her life. First she said HEY to all her kinky friends. Then she said goodbye to them, with literal tears in her eyes, 'cause she really truly deeply liked them as people, it's just it was time for her to take another path. She traveled out to the countryside, pissed on her sicko uncle's grave and went around telling everybody what had happened to her, and eventually she, like, regurgitated it all for her mom and asked her if she'd really never seen the signs, couldn't she have been her brother's keeper or whatever? Then they fought. They cried and screamed, apologized and forgave each other, and that was literally the first step on her road to recovery. But it didn't stop there. So, this amazing woman started meditating. Then she discovered tantra. I mean, she realized you gotta bring mind and body together, right, but that's easier said than done! She realized meditation by itself doesn't cut it, because it's just about your upstairs, and that sex by itself doesn't cut it either because it's basically just about your downstairs. But tantra brings the two together. Five years ago that made a lot of sense to me. I told her, Hey, I'm interested in that too, 'cause every time I get intimately involved with someone it feels like I'm banging my head against the wall. And you know what? She said, Why don't you come along then? She was traveling to hippie communes all over the world, and she was just about to leave for Eskilstuna, Sweden. Come with me, she said. It's the biggest tantra festival in Scandinavia. No, I'm not up to it, I whined. You can do it, she said. Imagine, we'd only known each other for like a week. But she was at the point on her own spiritual journey where she was able to look at me with, like, total conviction through those amber eyes of hers and say, You can do it. And then it happened; that confidence seemed to flow from her eyes right into me, and I one hundred percent knew I could do it. We smashed the windows and I stepped out of my stuffy room. Then we went to her apartment because I didn't have a home anymore. I mean that's, like, a metaphor, I wasn't literally homeless. But this bit is totally, one hundred percent true: I went to her place, and on the bedside table there was this book called *Waking the Tiger—Healing Trauma*. And this is legit, okay: it was like we instantly went into this, like, cocoon state. In bed she showed me her stomach. Across her lower abs she had a tattoo that said WE ARE HUMAN BEINGS, NOT HUMAN DOINGS, and I kissed all the letters one at a time. She had a triskelion tattooed around her belly button, a memory of her BDSM days. I kissed that too. She was so sensitive, the tantra breathing started all by itself. First you inhale in regular ashtanga style, a deep breath in through the nose, then exhale through the mouth, letting out a bunch of noise. I was super shocked, the sound came out so suddenly. Like, omg, did she just have an orgasm from me kissing her? But you know what? The sound that freaked me out at first got all my Kundalini energies moving. My pussy started, like, pulsating, and it rippled through my body and I started shivering all over. And we kissed. She only had to touch my vulva, her hands light as feathers, and gently raise her fingers, and I came. After that it never happened that quickly again. But we had that shared moment. I told her I loved her; it meant I loved everybody, and she totally got it. Then we set off for Eskilstuna. When we got there, the air was thick with incense, guys strumming the guitar, people standing there like statues, hugging each other for minutes at a time. I got that they all knew each other, that they're all part of the same tantra family and that there's nothing wrong with me, but I was, like, totally devastated that they didn't hug me that long. You know, I was so hungry when I went there. I wanted someone to, like, hold me for the rest of my life. Thank god my new girlfriend took good care of me. She whispered: I'll be your doula, honey, now you can give birth to the real you, you can be the person you truly are. Then we all held hands and sang *I'm Beautiful* with guitars and lutes and flutes and maracas. Whenever we got the chance we had a love shower, where blessing runs off your fingers like raindrops, it comes out of your mouth in a whisper—and when there are like a hundred of you, give or take, then I guarantee you, it works. You'd have to be made of concrete to look cynically at all that love. I learned a ton of important things on that course, like, you know, that you shouldn't beg for love and that all desire is just pushing and pulling away, that there needs to be, like, a balance. But now I can't remember a lot of it. I haven't practiced those skills since, and it's an attitude you gotta work at to keep it keep alive, it's a lifetime job. *Be true to your heart,* right? As soon as I got home, I flushed it all straight down the john. I fell head over heels for another troglodyte—un-fucking-believable. This man-sized prick managed to empty me of all my burgeoning tantric wisdom, and I was such a stupid dumbass that I let it happen. I totally forgot that we can *all* penetrate the universe, that all we need is our breath, 'cause at the time all I wanted was dick, dick and more dick. But that's another story. I'm getting to the stuff I use at the moment, the tender buttons. They were handed out to us on the last day of the course in some kind of ritual—and these aren't the kind of buttons you have on your clothes, by the way, these are magic pills. I'm trying to bring us back to the softness—which is still the wrong word, but whatever—and in a minute I'll get on to why my girlfriend got such kicks out of terry towels. On the tantra course, she had this white terry towel, and there's nothing weird about that, right, the best towels are made of terry cloth. But, like, she didn't just use it to dry herself or to lie on during a massage or oil therapy; she wanted to be taken through the towel—like, literally, tantrically. I cottoned on to her fetish on the second-to-last night at the course, in one of the love lounges we had after a cacao ceremony. There was a real bacchanal going on, and I moved from one cluster of bodies to the next, looking, touching a little, kissing, but I wasn't one hundred percent focused 'cause all the time I was peering through the dim looking for my friend. I really needed to see someone familiar, to create a safe space for myself. Anyways, eventually I found her. She was in one of the clusters of bodies,

legs here and there, lots of heavy petting (because, alongside penetration, oral sex was totally off-limits)—safe sex only, right? I
lay down next to her so our heads were next to each other. There
was a commotion going on between her legs and she was totally
out of her mind, then suddenly she kinda woke up and looked at
me with those amazing amber eyes of hers and whispered in Finnish (because there weren't any other Finnish speakers around),
Honey, would you do me a favor? Would you pick up my towel
and lay it over me? she asked. Then would you lie on top of me, if
that's okay? I was kinda speechless, skin contact is the be-all and
end-all in these circles, but I did as she said. The guys doing the
petting made space and carried on dry-humping each other on
another mattress. Then my friend whispered to me, said she's so
sensitive these days that, like, the lint on the towel, those awesome
little loops of toweling, they feel really intense against her skin.
She told me she sometimes runs her fingertips across a terry towel
for hours at a time, against the grain of the fabric, then gradually
spreads her hand out and pushes it forward, keeping the towel in
place by holding onto the hanger with her thumb and forefinger.
Then she gently pulls the hanger in the opposite direction to her
opened palm. The stretch of the fabric, the movement against the
grain, the tightness of the hanger, the softness of the towel. But
that softness isn't feather or down, it's not cotton or lamb's-wool
softness, there's a kinda harshness about it, you know? The sensation is, like, holistic. So anyways, I lay down on top of her and she
grabbed me as if I was, like, a cello or something and started sorta
playing me. Real small movements, so I could only just feel it, but

she was in a state of *o-o-o-overwhelming* desire, abso-fucking-lutely there in the moment. Then she asked me to pour water over her pussy from a bottle, and I did it, and the water first soaked into the towel above her vulva, then trickled down along her slit, and right then she started moaning, she pulled me back on top of her, placed a hand against my neck and pressed my lips against hers and shouted right into my mouth. Our shakti and shiva combined so that the whole mattress started shaking! And then there were the tender buttons. This was the day we were leaving. We all got together for this closing ceremony kinda thing, we gathered all the energy we'd created and did a spiral dance where everybody meets everybody else face-to-face, eye-to-eye. And after the dance we swallowed the buttons, the tender buttons. A cool white little pill that you pop into your mouth, then think about the truth that has, like, brightened and opened up to you on the course, the truth we all wanted to take home with us. That's what we were thinking about when we popped those pills, then we turned and said it out loud to whoever was standing next to us.

And now I'll return to my own voice, Doctor, all at once, as my story and my strength are almost at an end. There was an Icelandic man standing next to me, and I'd rubbed an entire tub of coconut oil into his body at a tantric massage workshop a few days earlier. I swallowed my tender button, gripped this stranger's hands and looked right into his inconsequential eyes. And in Finnish I whispered a sentence to him that I've never said to anyone since. Not even to you.

[17 MINUTES 58 SECONDS]

BAND-AID MAN & ROBIN GAYLE WRIGHT PENN

Soon after returning from the tantric course, I found a new lover who thought he was my Band-Aid Man but who was no such thing. He wouldn't believe anything I said to him, and instead turned everything on its head. He was large and furry, and I found it hard to be on my guard with him; at first I didn't want to be on my guard because it was nice to sink into that large, furry body of his, it was warm there, like being wrapped in a sheepskin, until eventually it got too hot. Of course, I knew that a lover who turned everything I said on its head could be dangerous, but I didn't care. And I used to have a friend (emphasis on the past tense) who was able to interpret these upside-down words. My friend returned these words to their rightful places, to the things I'd once said and meant, so that I could understand them again. But once back in the right order, the words felt restless, unwilling to stay in place. At the first opportunity they tried to unwind themselves and return to their topsy-turvy positions because they found all other positions too boring. On one occasion, my friend berated me. "Natalia, listen to me. If you spend your time cooing at him, *Sweetie darling, let's go to the spa, let's kiss under the waterfall,* and he shouts back at you, *Wash your mouth, you slut, then wash it again and again and again*, that's no basis for a loving relationship. You're not living in the same reality. You shouldn't break yourself. No lover is worth that, not even this one. Come on, let's walk down to the beach, go swimming, the water is still warm, we'll take a dip in the sea and have pancakes afterward, comfort food.

You have to learn to survive on your own. You have to learn to place pleasure on your own skin, to put candy in your mouth by yourself. Don't ever expect anyone else to do anything for you!" But at this point I stopped understanding. The returned upturned words started twisting again, and all I could hear was my lover's voice and my own voice, our voices ringing in an incessant loop in my head. I decided to try by myself, to remove myself from danger. I'd read somewhere that literature helps us to live a better life, and so I went to the library and took out a book. It was black, the dust jacket was missing, the author's name stood on the spine in white and the book's title in blue lettering. The title contained only one word, which pleased me immensely, and that word had only seven letters, and that pleased me too. The name was at once abstract and concrete, it didn't give me any clue as to what I might find inside the book, and I thought this was a good sign: the book might surprise me. So I allowed the book the chance to help me. Everything started off very promisingly. I read, I was excited, for a moment I forgot about everything else, my libido, my desires, the burning sensation and the pain running through me like an electric shock for which there are no words, the pain that if I were asked to measure it on a scale of one to ten I would always answer IT'S A TEN even if it wasn't true because otherwise I would have felt even stupider than I already did. And so I read, the way healthy people read books. They engage with strange, foreign worlds, become excited by them, and they are surprised only because the world opening up in front of them is so different from their own world, they are nourished by carefully crafted observations, the kind of observations they themselves would never be able to make because their time is a time of life, not of writing. But they know how to read, god they're skillful readers! They carry books with them wherever they go, in their bags and backpacks, they take them out on the streetcar and dive into them, and that's what I did too, suddenly I too was a healthy person diving into a book on a streetcar. I felt a tremendous sense of happiness because the strange words carried me with them the way they carried other people too, people better than me. I enjoyed the way my interest, that misshapen, unruly gadget, tirelessly followed the running text from one line to the next. But I jumped too soon. My original sin. I always count my chickens when I shouldn't. I think a fleeting moment is a permanent truth and I count my chickens. I convince myself that I'll be happy for the rest of my life, certain that sorrow has crushed me for good, I believe that what I feel at any given moment is true, though it's just a flicker in time, and only writing can make it real. So I read this book and I was in ecstasy because I was suddenly outside my own body, I had turned into a reader whose thoughts can be moved and shaped, when suddenly without any advance warning came a sentence, this sentence, a sentence that stopped everything dead: *Punch me, and I'll thump you back a few times if you don't believe me.* And at that very moment as I read those words, the pain running through me like an electric shock wrenched me out of the orbit along which I was slowly but surely moving toward a Significant and Full Life, the kind of life other people live, smoother, more complete people than me. Over decades they have grown, spiritually exceeding themselves in their healthy, boring relationships, they know how to curl up against one another and separate from one another just as easily as I know how to burn the rotten, rickety bridges of my own relationships; they are always upbeat, going somewhere, moving forward, toward their objectives, a destination, they sit in trams, buses, trains, ferries, airplanes, on the backseats of cars or in the passenger seat, reading their books until their eyes dry in their sockets. I was so envious of them! I wanted to push a razor blade into the whites of their eyes! Though, of course, it wasn't their fault that my progress had run into a brick wall with the sentence *Punch me, and I'll thump you back a few times if you don't believe me*, with which Band-Aid Man, who wasn't a Band-Aid but wanted to believe he was, forced his way into my mind, great, full-length, and furry. I was quivering from head to toe. I had to put the book away, my hands were shaking so much. I stepped off the tram because I needed immediate help. I decided to call a helpline, and you can't make a call like that with other people listening. There I stood, that radiant late summer's day, as I tried to remind myself that ultimately this is only about death: every summer sadistically offers up its beautiful body simply so that we may experience *memento mori* and so on. I stood at the tram stop and tapped in the number, and a woman's voice answered at the other end: "Helpline. How can I help?" Because it was a woman's voice, I stupidly imagined that she and I might share a similar reality, that we'd read the same books, watched the same films, listened to the same songs, visited the same exhibitions, fallen in love with the same kind of people, allowed the same kind of people to hurt us—because why else would she be working at a helpline unless she was like me? Anyway, because I still suspected (or perhaps I should say my rationale suspected) that there was no way she could possibly be exactly like me, I didn't begin my confession by talking about the man like a large furry sheepskin who wouldn't leave me alone but who popped into my head in the most extraordinary places. I began by talking about Sean Penn's ex-wife, whose name used to be Robin Gayle Wright Penn and was now simply Robin Gayle Wright. You see, I told the lady at the helpline, Robin dropped the Penn from her name and her identity. What use was Penn to her now? What use are men anyway, or men's names; isn't our own name good enough? I spoke to the helpline lady about the film *Loved* starring Sean Penn and his then-wife Robin. In fact, Sean Penn (second name on the credit list) was such a big star at the time that he got his name and face on the posters for the film, even though his brief appearance at the beginning of this hundred-minute movie lasts only about five minutes and some seconds. The broken man that Penn portrays drones on about the magnets that we humans are supposed to be, we are like magnets placed next to one another, he repeats, and he asks for help, but he is beyond help—and it's no wonder, because he talks nothing but undiluted pseudo-psychological bullshit. Neither money nor hugs will make his misery disappear, though he gets both from the lawyer played by William Hurt (first name on the credit list), whose good-hearted sense of charity toward the unknown and mentally unstable has now duly been presented to viewers. Do you remember, I asked the lady, do you remember the other broken soul in the film, Sean's wife Robin, who plays the role of Hedda? Robin/Hedda (twelfth name on the credit list) spends the entire film weeping, smiling, swimming, speaking and prancing through Los Angeles barefoot like a country girl. When the film was first released, Robin and Sean had been married for about a year, and they would eventually divorce after fourteen years of marriage. I didn't ask the helpline lady whether she had seen *Loved*, it didn't even occur to me to ask her because I assumed that all women who were alive in 1997 would have seen that infuriating courtroom drama *and* that everyone was thinking about Sean Penn's previous marriage to Madonna as they watched it. Do you remember the baseball bat, I asked the telephone lady, do you remember the nicknames, Poison Penns, S&M? Do you remember the lamp, the electrical cord used to tie the songstress up, do you remember the gag used to shut her mouth, do you remember the police patrol called to their Malibu residence? Do you remember, I continued my line of questioning, how Robin Gayle Wright Penn's Hedda stood up in the courtroom and defended her violent ex-husband, played by Anthony Lucero (fourth name on the credit list)? Do you remember Hedda's outburst? *He is my arm. He is my leg. Are you over your arm? Are you over your leg? I don't want to be over my arm! I don't want to be over my leg!* I repeated Hedda's lines to the helpline lady, the lines that Hedda tearily spluttered to her lawyer sister, lines that became seared into my mind in 1997, a time when I hadn't yet begun to chart my own experiences with dangerous lovers. Instead of Robin's face, I saw Madonna's face, then instead of Madonna's face I saw Robin's face, one after the other, just as looking at the rabbit/duck illusion we sometimes see a rabbit, sometimes a duck. More specifically, in my mind's eye I saw Madonna from the time of the *Something to Remember* album, I heard the track "Live to Tell" from that album while onscreen Hedda/Robin/Madonna claimed—under oath—that there was really never any danger, because when her husband pressed the pillow over her face he left enough room for her to breathe. The helpline lady listened attentively, the way you're supposed to listen to a complete stranger in need of help. I was just about to reach the original point, the sentence *Punch me, and I'll thump you back a few times if you don't believe me* and the sudden electric pain it caused, which sent me hurtling toward a tingling lovelessness, when my phone's battery died.

And that was that.

[13 MINUTES 41 SECONDS]

Natalia's problems were not unique, but the manner in which she chose to deal with her pain was starting to concern me more and more. We spent three whole weeks dealing with the auditory recordings she had made, after which she obediently packed her recording device into its bag, as we'd agreed. She handed over the Philips 0005 mini-cassettes, three in total, to me.

As I listened to these recordings, I gradually began to understand the direction in which Natalia was heading, though she went to a great deal of trouble to conceal this obvious matter. I noted the way in which she embedded crucial interpretative clues into her stories and presented them as nothing but tragicomic curiosities. She talked around matters, and in doing so she revealed, either intentionally or unintentionally, her most painful wounds. For instance, she introduced the theme of *vagina dentata* into her story about the man with the diagonal testicle, a theme that in the post-Jungian tradition invokes the Terrible Mother in whose vagina lives a fish with razor-sharp teeth. Her story about the terry-cloth fetish featured a mother-daughter conflict motivated by incest, though she presented this as part of her tantra friend's backstory. And it was not lost on me to whom she was referring with the helpline lady in her story about Band-Aid Man.

Was Natalia knowingly throwing these insinuations around, in other words, was she testing my professionalism, or were these myths and archetypes speaking through her? If the latter, as I was beginning to suspect, the woman lying on my couch was a sensation whose treatment deserved an article of its own, if not an entire book.

Once I realized this, I was filled with joy verging on euphoria, the kind of euphoria I had last felt in the early stages of my PhD research, back when everything was still possible. The idea of "working through" this material, as Natalia had boastfully suggested before our little listening exercise, no longer felt beyond the bounds of possibility.

What's more, I began to view Natalia's earlier exercises in a new light, as if this recent observation put them in a different perspective. When Natalia variously mutilated the female body, reducing it to simply a mouth, a head or a torso, what she didn't say was *whose* body she was tearing to pieces. Perhaps Natalia's obsessive desire to equate sex and violence wasn't about domestic violence, as I had previously assumed, but rather it revealed a murderous lust driving her in a wholly different direction. Yes indeed, we were now hurtling toward the original of all traumas, the unresolved Oedipal conflict, the stage upon whose boards trod *mētēr āmētōr*, the mother who is not a mother. This was Natalia's destination, and the journey there clearly terrified her, and for that reason she sugarcoated everything with the most shameless elements of fiction.

You may be wondering how I had the conviction to draw these far-reaching conclusions at such an early stage. Transparency is part of my professional ethics, so I am happy to reveal my thinking. Layer therapy is a useful form of treatment partly because it produces results more quickly than traditional psychotherapy. Seven layering sessions is equivalent to fourteen traditional therapy sessions, a matter to which the incontrovertible data presented in my PhD attests.

Further support for my intuition is provided by years of clinical practice during which I have learned that, the more emancipated the woman, the more likely she is to try to sew up the gateway to her inner self with phallic metaphors. Thus, she is able to withstand the subconscious anguish caused by the unresolved triangle drama of her childhood. In this respect, Natalia's early fantasies about gay pornography are revealing. In fact, the inordinate idolization of her father, in which Natalia took solace time and time again, is evidence of the same underlying problem. She spoke of her father in radiant terms when she recounted the mystery of the hidden pornographic magazine, while she presented the epistle about the cheating husband bribing his lovers with jewelry by the Sent sisters as further evidence of her father's moral superiority. Bringing the tape recorder into our sessions was a

phallic gesture in its own right, but Natalia wouldn't be Natalia
had she not immediately emasculated the device by referring to
her vagina as an "eel trap." Here we see the fundamental genius of
layer therapy: it accelerates the transmogrification of things into
other things and thus speeds up the appearance of symbiotic relationships, the threshold upon which traditional therapy flounders
for years at a time.

Will these arguments allay your doubts?

Shall I now show you where poor Natalia was heading?

"Natalia," I said as gently as I could when I switched on my
Olympus recorder, equipped with an eight-gigabyte internal
memory, and which I'd brought from home and now placed on
the lace tablecloth where Natalia's tape recorder had been before.
"Thank you for this final story. Allow me to read aloud a sentence
I noted down while listening to your recording. You said that
your former friend advised you as follows: *You have to learn to place
pleasure on your own skin, to put candy in your mouth by yourself.* Those
are wise words. I think this quotation is one of the key turning
points in your life story. I believe we're approaching the heart
of the issue. It can be immeasurably difficult to enjoy one's own
body, if you haven't been encouraged to do so from a young age."

I could feel in my bones the electric charge that suddenly filled
the room. Natalia, who only a moment ago had been lying on the
couch as relaxed as a seal basking in the sunlight on a rock by the
shore, suddenly tensed, her body as taut as a violin string.

I continued as I had planned, releasing the clusters of questions
I'd been preparing over a long time. "As a child, did you feel you

were supported in trying to love yourself? Did your mother love herself? Did she respect her own body? Did she ever touch you tenderly? Did she look at you acceptingly?"

In general, I leave the client space to glide here and there, to grasp one mental association after the other, but this time I tried a different tactic. The exercise I wanted Natalia to complete required some amount of preparation, and for this reason I pulled back the heavy velvet curtains from our stage right at the outset. "When you were speaking to the helpline lady in your last story, who were you actually addressing?"

Natalia remained silent for a long while. When she finally opened her mouth, her voice sounded dull, peppered with stifled rage, as though she were speaking from the bottom of a well that had dried up long ago.

"My mother hated my sexuality," she whispered. "That's why I moved in with my grandmother when I was in high school. You see, I quickly learned that I was never going to lose my virginity in my own home, that I would die an old spinster if I stayed there."

I didn't have the heart to tell her that few of us ever lose our virginity in our childhood home, especially while our parents are there. I allowed Natalia to continue opening up.

"Like everybody else at that age, I tried to start dating," she said. "I wanted to take my first boyfriends home. And I did! I smuggled them into my bedroom, that is, into the attic, as any of my classmates would have done. But, Doctor, imagine what my dear old mother did? She would come up with the stupidest reasons to appear in the hallway and listen, to sneak a step higher, another, another, until finally she was standing behind my door, craning her neck. Such was the magnetic force that my first boyfriends and I gave off!"

It couldn't be a coincidence that Natalia used the reference to magnets, because only a moment ago she had ridiculed Sean Penn's movie character for using the same metaphor. Now Natalia's voice, still blurry with anger, sounded so genuine that this couldn't possibly be a throwaway, ironic comment. Did she really believe that we humans are like magnets placed next to one another?

As for the burgeoning desires of young lovers, from my own experience I would say that it only feels like a magnetic encounter to them. For older people like us, it's largely just amusing. Of course, in our culture we idealize young love, and that's the way people want to keep it. Silky soft, toothpaste-fresh, as beguiling as whale song. It is three-dimensional like the View-Master reels about the life of Jesus: the waters part, people rise up to heaven, but there isn't a single stereoscopic image depicting the experiential moment of doubt.

"No, maybe my mother wasn't like that after all," Natalia said after a moment's contemplation. "My sex life distressed her so much that she didn't hang about in the hallway. She bounded up the stairs, wrenched the door open immediately after knocking on it, without waiting for permission to enter. She surprised me and my boyfriend with hot chocolate—that's what she did. There she stood, two steaming mugs of hot chocolate on a tray . . ."

Natalia's voice no longer echoed up the walls of the well. Now

the words were like red-hot lava that she belched out in bursts,
with all the force of her body quivering with rage.

"My mother steps into the room. I stop mid-blowjob and peek
out from beneath the duvet. The boy is in shock and grabs a pillow to cover his face. I look at my mother from between the boy's
legs. The surprise feels dizzying, I'm in such disbelief. I remember my mother's pinched smile. I remember her face, which she
managed to twist into a smile. I'm surprised she didn't give us a
knowing wink. So you and I are in the same boat, eh, she might as
well have said. Been there, done that, nudge-nudge wink-wink!
You'll soon get the hang of it! Take a break, kids, have a nice cup
of *chocolat chaud*."

Natalia was breathing intensely, fumbling for her next
thought. Was it true? She decided it was and let herself go.

"My mother was determined to ruin my fledgling sex life. It's
as simple as that. One time she said she was worried I would contract an STD or that I'd end up pregnant. She never mentioned
condoms, as normal mothers would if they were worried about
such things. She talked about her own fears. She said she was trying to be both discreet and honest. But she was neither! If she'd
been honest, she would have admitted she was worried about one
thing and one thing only: that I might enjoy sex more than she
did. And, oh, how I enjoyed it! I flourished. I grew into a woman
and my mother shriveled into a lying scarecrow. That's why I
moved to my grandmother's house in the nearby town as soon as
I started high school."

Natalia paused, but only for a moment. She wanted to seal her memories so that she would never again have to touch them with words. It was as though this final sentence pressed my cheek—not her mother's—against the floor of the boxing ring. "Let that teach you a thing or two about motherly love, Doctor!"

I was ecstatic. My methods were working more effectively than I ever dared to hope. We had reached a crossroads in the therapy process, the very core of the emotional displacement, a moment I would not allow myself to waste. My task was to guide Natalia, cautiously but surely, toward the next exercise in which she would be able to tell me in her own words what it was that she ultimately blamed her mother for.

"I have an idea," I said, and began softening the ground where I hoped Natalia would step. "In your story about the Terry-Towel Fetish, you claim you are bad at impersonating people. But I don't believe you. In fact, I suspect impersonation gives you considerable satisfaction. I've noted that you take great inspiration from works of art. You love paintings, cinema, literary art, just like I do. So I suggest, therefore, that you choose a work of art that's important to you and experiment with it. Submerge yourself in the work and make it your own. Quite literally."

RECOVERY PROGRAM
WEEK 8

Instruction: Imitate an artistic master of your choice.
Maintain a focus on the topic of motherly love.

"Today I'd like to talk to you about Niki de Saint Phalle's work *My Men*, created in 1994 when Niki was sixty-four years old. In 1994 I was almost fifty years younger than her, and back then I'd never heard of her. Specifically, I'm going to talk about her series *Californian Diary*. When I first saw it in 2014 it truly shocked me, because exactly twenty years earlier—that is, in the same year as Niki—I was making tableaux like that too. Naturally, my technique wasn't quite as assured as hers, she'd had time to think things through, to find those lines, those colors, to fall in love and experience betrayal, while for me all that was going to happen much later. My men, if they can be called men at all, came into my life after the nth wave of feminism had washed over me without leaving a trace and the conversation had already moved on, the way it always does, whereas what I wanted to talk about had already become the stuff of museums. I was in a museum, it was 2014, and I was staring at one of the frames from *Californian Diary*, a tableau called *My Men*, and I felt suddenly dizzy and tearful because twenty years had elapsed since 1994 and twenty years ago, blissfully unaware of Niki, I was producing Niki-esque tableaux in my grandmother's living room, because my need for self-expression was insatiable and I harbored dreams of becoming an artist. *My Men*, drawn, colored, and above all written by Niki de Saint Phalle (who by this point was dead, just as I too would die sooner or later), was in a museum, Niki herself was a museum item just like *My Men*, and I couldn't think of any way to overcome my shock than to trace Niki's handwritten story on my own sheet of paper, a story that wasn't a story at all but a torrent of curlicue, almost coquettish statements surrounded by all kinds of naïve illustrations. I drew things like this in 1994 too! But, of course, my works weren't displayed in a museum. I was just a visitor in this museum, I stood in front of Niki's work and cried inside. I decided to take revenge on her for her age and skill, for the fact that back in 1994 I wasn't her but me, by copying those silly, straight-talking words in my own handwriting on my own little piece of paper. But I didn't have any paper. And I didn't want to ask the museum for paper, because if they'd had any paper it would likely have been the wrong kind, it would have borne the museum's logo or come with lines to help guide your writing, and I needed a blank sheet. And this is why I went back to the museum the next day. I arrived as soon as the doors opened at ten a.m. As I hoped, there was nobody else in the room where *My Men* was displayed. I had exactly the same size of paper as Niki had used in *Californian Diary*, and beneath it I had a piece of cardboard the same size, which served as my table. I had different paints, pencils in different colors, and with that I started copying it. I'll show you my work soon, and I warn you it's not identical to *My Men*, not remotely, but it's not supposed to be. There's only one Niki and only one Natalia, and there's a certain difference between them; who am I to try to erase it? But first, a matter that disturbs me. If I'd had a father who sexually abused me, as Niki did—and that's why she felt the desire to throw darts into the pictures she'd drawn of men and displayed these in museums too, because for her all men were her father, she took a gun and shot at paintings and statues that were all ultimately men and fathers, and not just men and fathers but mothers too and Niki herself, everyone who had allowed this to happen, and she took those paintings and statues, complete with bullet holes, into museums and asked viewers to throw darts at them, to shoot them as in a grotesque arcade game, as though the viewer could imagine anyone at all on the target, a real asshole, someone who had really hurt the person throwing the dart, though in reality the target was nobody but Niki's father, who had—and now I'll have to use my imagination because I don't know and I don't want to know the sordid details—somehow stripped his eleven-year-old child's lower body naked and stuck at the very least his forefinger into his prepubescent daughter's dry little vagina . . . So, if I'd had a father like this, I would never have spoken so admiringly about the monster called Gilles de Rais. But Niki de Saint Phalle did.

I don't care how great a war hero Rais was (he wasn't actually that great; he led a small troop of men in the Hundred Years' War as a general of Jeanne d'Arc), I don't care what noble lineage he had (he certainly had that, but is that really such an achievement? I think not), he was also and above all a child rapist and child murderer, six-year-old boys being to his mind the greatest delicacy of all. What's more, he was related to Niki through her father, so we know where her father had inherited those genes. One could imagine that through her art Niki might want to throw darts not only at her mother and father and herself, but also at images of Gilles de Rais; but instead she said that Gilles de Rais *interested her,* that the conflicted character of Gilles de Rais was *interesting.* I find this disgusting, and I will say the following about child molestation: it is quite simply repulsive. When I was five years old, I'd never heard the words 'pedophilia' or 'incest,' and neither did I understand that there were people in this world, mostly fathers, who could actually do something like that to a child, but that's what Niki de Saint Phalle's father did to her. What I did know at five years old was that between a father and daughter there is not only love but a chasm of love, something that doesn't exist between a mother and daughter or between a mother and father. One summer's day, my father and I came home from the village. We'd been food shopping together. I organized our few items in the basket with my five-year-old's sense of order, at my father's behest I fetched things from the shelves and learned to read at the same time, I read the letters

EMMENTAL and placed a chunk of cheese in the basket, and I was so proud of myself I could have burst. We didn't buy very many things, just enough that we could carry home on our bikes: in the basket attached to the rack of my father's bike, where he put the milk, cheese, bread and two bottles of beer, one for my mother and one for himself, and the basket tied to the handlebars of mine, where I put what I considered the greatest treat of all, a Ukrainian salad that was at once tart, salty, sweet and sour. We pedaled back home side by side, my father on the side nearest the traffic because he was an adult, and me on the sidewalk because I was a child. And I shouted to him: 'Look, Daddy, I'm riding abreast of you!' I wasn't using training wheels anymore, we'd taken them off at the beginning of the summer, I could already ride a bike properly and so I rode alongside him, just as I'd said. But once I said those words, once I said *I'm riding abreast of you*, I sped up, because I wanted to stay abreast of him, and I pedaled with all my energy, without braking, until suddenly the handlebars flipped as I lost control of the bike. The Ukrainian salad flew in an arc from the basket to the asphalt and the glass jar shattered, and I too flew in an arc over the handlebars and landed on the asphalt, right on my chin, and, like my chin, the back of my left hand and the front of my right hand hit the street at the same time. The velocity was so great, I ground a few centimeters along the asphalt, and there was a lot of blood and cuts and scratches along my chin and hands. I screamed like a little beast, I thought I was going to die, the pain was so great that I wanted to die. My father moved our bikes to one side and picked me up. He talked to me calmly as he carried me in his strong arms, our house wasn't very far away. My mother ran out into the street as we approached. She had heard my screams all the way back at the house, I had a loud voice, the loudest in the village, everybody knew where I was at all times—my laughter even scared off the crows. My mother disinfected my wounds and checked that all my teeth were still in place. My father went back to fetch the bikes and collect the groceries from the roadside. He gathered the remains of the Ukrainian salad and the shards of glass into a plastic bag, and we didn't have any salad for a while. I'm not sure quite when I realized it, whether it happened at the precise moment I was lying on the pavement, my chin bloodied, or whether it happened earlier as I was flying through the air, or later on when I was at home, but be that as it may, I realized with the lightning clarity that only a five-year-old can have that I'd fallen off my bike because I'd said to my father *I'm riding abreast of you*. I had crossed the invisible chasm, the barrier erected between a father and daughter, and which must remain erect lest we find ourselves at the cusp of moral transgression. I had spoken to my father about *breasts*, things both of us had, I had breasts and my father had breasts, but only my mother had breasts that mattered, breasts that I had inadvertently invoked in speaking about riding abreast of my father. My mother had big tits from which I'd suckled five years ago, but those breasts didn't belong to me anymore. So when I was riding abreast of my father—and said it out loud—I had in fact committed several misdemeanors, and as a result I was doomed to fall and injure myself. I had shifted my mother's breast, the only breast of any significance in our small family, and placed it between my father and me, by shouting out *I'm riding abreast of you* I'd made my father my mother and my mother a means of transport. I had turned my father into something he was not and could never be, I had made him an enormous gland secreting fatty milk, and I had ridden on that gland, my legs astride it like Baron von Münchhausen on his cannonball. No wonder I'd fallen off! With that in mind, I want to say that even a small child should have the wherewithal to demand that Niki de Saint Phalle should have unequivocally condemned Gilles de Rais, her great-great-great-great-great-great-grandfather or whatever he was, and she should certainly not have intoned, her voice fulsome and pretentious, that Gilles de Rais was 'interesting.' Let me show you the reproduction I made of the written sections of *My Men*. Here it is:

Dear Diary,

① I have always chosen men who would betray me like my father

You are a Strange Bird
Sexy Snakes

② I was seeking to be Betrayed again to prove that men would always Betray

③ I chose interesting often brilliant men all of them womenizers. I was attracted to them for what appeared to be Strength, Selfconfidence, Freedom, even for their Rapid undressing techniques . which helped free me. Being raised in a convent it's difficult not to be overly modest and inhibited.

④ What were they addicted to? Admiration of other men for their numerous women?? Mother? Fear of Women? Weak Ego? competition? Like Football players always wanting to score?
Desire for Control? (yes)
NON

⑤ These Men loved me, excited my mind, inspired me, but I never entirely revealed myself to them. I remained an Enigma. My Work came first. My protection independance, Chère inner joy beyond what they could provide. My Men (these beasts) were my muses. The suffering they inflicted and the vengeance I took nourished My Art for Many Years.

I Thank Them.

I'm addicted to humour.
I'll forgive you anything because you make me laugh.

URGENT call me right away
or I kill you

California Mountains

I had a weird dream last night
you were a gorilla.
In my work I often portray men
as animals. Why?
Eat or (and) be eaten.
Fly away with me
MeRci My MeN My ANiMAL
OUi
I like turtles   yes
                        maybe?
I dreamt I was
        Lady Godiva
                        personel
            What is it
                all about?

⑥ My Revenge
on these men
abandonment I ended
Relationships suddenly
I was Ruthless. GOODBYE!
Desolée salaud ordure je me
                    Vengerais

Thank you for the Flowers
Stop hopping into every bed
    You stupid kangaroo
You remind me of a cow not
                        a Bull
    HELP! You? Me?
              Me? You?
Silly me
Who is the Bear?
    Who is the Seal?

(7) Thank God I am no longer attracted to those types of men. Deliverance at last! Now I know I'd prefer Someone who Took a long Time undressing me...

What do you think of this, my dearest doctor? My father was nothing like Niki de Saint Phalle's monster father, and I'm sure my lovers were nothing like Niki's lovers. Maybe one of the men in my life was a full-blooded womanizer, but only one—which is quite few, if you ask me. I can't relate to Niki's life other than through her handwriting, which bears a striking resemblance to my own, which during my teenage years started to grow in size, becoming increasingly florid, wild and unbridled, which is probably why I feel an irresistible desire to reproduce Niki's writing. Precisely that, to *reproduce*, exactly as it is. Tell me, Doctor, why I don't need to turn these words upside down? *I have never chosen men who betray me*, which is just about right, assuming betrayal is understood as infidelity. Why do I feel a compulsion to write *I have always chosen men who would betray me*, and why on earth should I wish, as I imitate Niki by drawing my pen in her footsteps, to

insert my very own, good and just father into that scenario, that
rogues' gallery of despicable traitors? I feel the urge to write,
again and again, the phrase *who would betray me like my father*
because he chose my big-chested mother over me, which of course
is perfectly normal, that's the way it should be. And my mother
chose him, my just and big-chested mother who during the daytime would have given her life for me. But only during the day. I
guess if I were to leap from your couch, run outside and conduct
a quick straw poll, asking passersby, 'Was your childhood happy
or unhappy?,' the vast majority would answer along the lines of
'There were happy days and unhappy days in my childhood.'
God, how blissful it would be to be able to answer like that! The
idea that there were whole days full of happiness, full, happy days.
Cumulus-cloud days, tiger-ice-cream days, forest-adventure
days, cheese-sandwiches-wrapped-in-wax-paper days. But in my
childhood, every day was only half filled with happiness. The
other half was overflowing with sorrow. Only the days when my
father was out of town were exclusively filled with happiness, and
even those were tinged with an inharmonious sadness, because all
the while I missed my father terribly; yet while I missed him, I
feared his return. I loved him with every fiber of my body, every
day of my life! On the days he was traveling, I placed my love in
a matchbox lined with cotton wool. The tiny glass bead, into
which I imagined transferring all the love I felt toward my father,
that glass bead, which my father had brought me from one of his
trips, was cool and smooth, and if you picked it up between your
thumb and forefinger and held it in front of your eyes, as I did

many times on the days my mother and I were alone in the house, I was sent hurtling into space, out amid the stardust and distant galaxies, because the universe beyond the earth was right there inside the bead. *I was seeking to be betrayed again to prove that men would always betray,* Niki wrote, and I wrote after her, and even as a child I knew, or at least my rational self knew, that my father didn't do it on purpose, he never knowingly put me in second place after my mother. But he couldn't help himself! Just as he couldn't help the fact that I was unable to sleep on the nights when he was home. I couldn't help it either. The person who could help it least of all was my energetic mother, whose unflagging sense of justice began to crack in those late hours of the evening, which is hardly surprising as I was an impossible child. Weepily I shouted for her to come to my bedside every ten minutes, thoroughly fed up with the situation myself, but I couldn't *not* shout out because if I'd been quiet for, say, fifteen minutes and pretended to be asleep, they would have closed my bedroom door and my world would have been destroyed irredeemably, as it had been destroyed many times before. They began preparing for this destruction at seven o'clock at the latest, when they gradually and seamlessly stopped being my mother and father. At seven o'clock one of them, usually my mother, started to speak in that tone of voice that meant I should start getting myself ready for bed and die there. She would talk about supper, brushing my teeth and putting my pajamas on, and because both my mother and father knew that I could easily spend hours on these three tasks, they began mentioning them earlier and earlier. You see, I remember the winter when they started encouraging me to get ready for bed at eight o'clock. But that was in the past. My father, who during the daytime was the best father in the world, positioned himself in front of the television during the time my mother raved on about going to bed. My father, whom I looked at defiantly as I walked past, as I slowly went through the same bag of tricks I used every evening, pretended not to understand what this playacting was all about. He just waited for the moment when he could give me a fatal kiss good night, the purpose of which was to stun me the way chloroform stuns a butterfly, so that he could do *it* with my mother, or get my mother to do *it*, something she didn't particularly like but which my father managed almost to hypnotize her into liking. If it really is the case that *I have always chosen men who would betray me like my father*, as Niki wrote, and as I wrote in imitation, the betrayal was right there in that magic power my father had, not out of spite or mischief but because he couldn't help himself. Enthralled by this magic, my mother lost all sense, all honor. When she was under that spell, she believed she actually wanted to lie beneath my father while he heaved on top of her. Sometimes she thought she wanted to get on top of him and imagine herself as a swan taking flight or a mole burrowing into the ground. There I stood at their bedroom door, staring at the dim bed where these two figures moved and moaned, until I realized that it was only my father making any noises. He was panting. In fact, years ago my mother told everyone that when she gave birth to me, she categorically did not scream like all the other women on the maternity ward, she pushed without making a sound, while the other women howled, yelled, shrieked, babbled and gurgled in pain. They shouted out in a language that not even god could understand. My mother had to listen to this cacophony before she eventually gave birth to me, during the birth and after the birth, and throughout her time on the ward. And it was on the first day, convulsed with contractions, that she decided she would give birth in utter silence. I pushed my way into the world slowly, with nothing but the force of inhalation and exhalation, and began breathing by myself, not without screaming, of course, because my mother's rule regarding not shrieking didn't apply to newborns. And I didn't stop shrieking as I grew up—as I said, I had the loudest voice in the village. In this respect, my mother and I were quite different. There's no way I could have pushed a baby out of my cupcake without screaming. I already knew this by the age of five. Babies are much bigger than cupcakes, at least my cupcake was smaller than even the teensy-weensiest premature baby you can imagine. This was one thing I couldn't get my head around. And if someone had stuck their willy into my cupcake, like my father did to my mother, I most certainly would not have been quiet about it. This was another thing I couldn't get my head around. On the other hand, I imagined that when a girl grows and becomes a woman, her cupcake must grow too; it must deepen inward the way arms and legs become visibly longer and stronger. But was my mother big enough inside? I didn't think so. Still, she was quiet. The more I thought about it, it should have been the other way around: my father should have been silent, not my mother, but it wasn't like that. Besides, by this point I had a new dilemma. I couldn't go back to my own bed because I was there already. If I'd gone back to my own bed to wait for *it* to be over, as I realized that, one way or another, *it* would be over at some point, it would have been tantamount to accepting the matter. But I didn't accept it! That's why I forced my way into my parents' bed, to put them off. I did it reluctantly. I wasn't afraid of my parents, but as I've already explained a million times, those two figures lurching in the bed, one of them panting, were not my parents. They had voluntarily relinquished their roles as my parents. I couldn't understand why. No, I'm talking nonsense again now. With my five-year-old's understanding of the world, I realized that for my father, as for all fathers in the world, this repugnant procedure was *essential*, whereas for my mother, as for all mothers in the world, the nauseating operation was not essential but *harmful*, or at the very least *unnecessary*. And still my mother succumbed to his magic and allowed herself to become enchanted. This was the third thing I couldn't get my head around. I couldn't fathom why my mother, who with the last remnants of her free will was still recognizably my mother at seven o'clock, would shoo me to bed while my father watched television with grim intensity. It would appear that my mother was already partially enchanted by this point, and this made her impatient with me. But at what point had it happened again? I never managed to catch my father in the act of enchanting her. He was always relaxed, happy and uncomplicated, except when he became angry, but that's another story. And because I was unable to affect the charade that started every evening at seven o'clock, because, even though I wanted to, I couldn't bellow *Don't let it happen tonight* at my mother as she hurried me to bed, there was only one option left: I couldn't allow night to fall. So I called my mother to my bedside for the seventh time, moaning 'I can't sleep,' 'I'm thirsty,' 'I need the toilet,' 'I'm hot,' 'I'm cold' or whatever it happened to be, I said whatever came into my mind, only deciding what to say once I had called my mother out of bed and heard her heavy steps behind my bedroom door. And she couldn't kill me, even if she'd wanted to, but each time she forced herself to ask, 'What's keeping you up, child? Why aren't you asleep?'

"This was my childhood, my dearest doctor. Every morning filled with joy and every evening filled with sorrow, except for the days when my father was out of town."

By now, I had to admit that Natalia's bringing the recorder to our sessions was a stroke of genius. The presence of the recorder clearly helped calm her down. In this respect, too, Natalia was different from most people I knew. For many people, the mere thought of listening to your own voice causes shivers of discomfort. Our voice sounds different, strange and yet so familiar when it comes from somewhere outside our own skull. When I was writing my PhD, I had to learn to cope with listening to my own speech. To my ear, it sounded like bleating, as fake as the talk of salvation by an overzealous preacher at an evangelist meeting. I had to ask my mentor what my voice really sounded like. My mentor said it was a perfect voice for therapy work, calm and clear, and though my ears told me otherwise, I simply had to accept it.

Natalia, on the other hand, seemed to love the sound of her

own voice, whether it came from her mouth or a tape recorder. And now she no longer had to worry about our conversations disappearing. The melodies of her stories, the minute shifts in tone, were all recorded for posterity. Now she could let herself be carried away by the flow and allow herself to look at her parents through the eyes of a disappointed five-year-old.

I was excited: the Saint Phalle story had proved my theory correct. Natalia's chronic yearning for men sprung from precisely the place I had suspected. It was a repetition of the pain she had experienced in childhood, an attempt to coax forth the frightening magic powers that she thought the male sex possessed. This was why she was prepared to give her body to anyone who cared to ask for it.

From the perspective of layer therapy, Natalia's libido was in a state of sclerosis. Despite its apparent activity, it was in fact dormant, hibernating like an ergot hiding within a grain of wheat, a parasite that would eventually multiply and destroy its host. The question is, which of them will win: the parasitic fungus or the nourishing wheat germ? Self-destructive in-and-out copulation or loving intercourse?

Natalia would have to boldly kick *pater omnipotens* off the stage and shove *mētēr āmētōr* out of the limelight. She had to find the courage to step out of the wings and onto the stage, straight into the dazzling glare of the lights, that magic place where she was enough for herself.

"I have a suggestion," I said as our session was drawing to a close. "As I see it, we have reached the point where we can now safely examine your inner self, your personal pleasure. In peace and quiet."

I held a probing pause, but because Natalia didn't respond, I continued. "In our first sessions, you produced a skillful drawing of an erect penis. How about for our next session you draw a picture of your own treasure trove, maybe using a handheld mirror to help you. Then you can construct a story around it. I take it you're familiar with *The Vagina Monologues*? Something like that, or something completely different. Whatever feels most natural for you."

Of course, Natalia's problems were not situated in her vagina, but I'd come to know her well enough that I could already see the benefits of this exercise; it was a potential breakthrough. Drawing is a meditative way of combining the hand and the mind, and Natalia desperately needed more exercises to strengthen these connections. When she re-created Niki de Saint Phalle's text in her own handwriting, she was liberated and could finally ask that most central question that puzzles all children: "Why did you make me only to abandon me?" How deep would Natalia be able to dig if she were to draw her own genitals, one detail at a time, taking as long as she needed? What would she ask of that orifice shrouded in folds, the place that conservative American ladies referred to as *down there*, a place that women can never see with their own eyes without the help of a mirror?

"It goes without saying, you don't have to show me your drawing," I said, as Natalia continued to respond to my suggestion with silence. "It would be your drawing, your secret. Together we can focus on the thoughts the process brings up."

Did Natalia, who didn't seem to have any inhibitions when it came to bawdy stories, the kind of stories with which she regaled me lying on my couch, suddenly consider my suggestion inappropriate? Lewd, even?

Once again, her reaction took me by surprise.

"I see, so you want me to draw my pussy? I've never thought of such a thing. Let me think about it."

Natalia began twiddling a lock of hair around her finger, as if this movement helped her to process my suggestion. "It's not a bad idea," she said eventually, her voice now curiously officious. "I can think it over, yes?"

I hadn't yet opened my mouth to assure her that she could think it over for as long as she wanted, when she suddenly made a countersuggestion.

"You don't yet know all sides of me," she began, to which I felt like responding that of course I didn't know all sides of her, she hardly knew them herself and that was presumably why she had sought my help, to acquaint herself with all sides of herself and to come to terms with them. "Is it all right," she asked coyly, "if I bring Veronica with me next time? And that we skip the exercise altogether?"

This was a move I hadn't anticipated. Was Veronica a new friend? Why on earth did she want to bring a friend to our session? Did she want the friend to tell me something that she either couldn't or wouldn't tell me herself? But Natalia no longer had any friends, or at least that's what she had told me. So who was this Veronica?

Or did Natalia mean that she would arrive at our session *as* Veronica, and if so, what would be the implications of that? If that was indeed what she meant, why didn't she simply ask, "Is it all right if I come as Veronica next time?"

"Who is Veronica?" I managed to ask.

"Veronica is Veronica," Natalia replied in a voice that made it clear that, for now, she wouldn't tell me any more.

I was about to say that unfortunately it's not possible to bring outsiders to our therapy sessions when Natalia leapt up from the couch and shrieked, "Oh no, I almost forgot!" Cursing to herself, she gathered her things, dashed into the hallway to pull on her coat and shoes, before briefly reappearing in the doorway to offer an explanation. "I went and booked a dentist appointment straight after our session. I forgot I'd have to bike there first!"

And with that Natalia disappeared from the room without so much as a goodbye.

A week later Veronica was lying on her back on the couch with the alarm clock on her stomach. Apparently this was enough for her, I thought to myself, an enormous black wig that she'd pulled over her head, the slightly ridiculous clothes with which she had transformed herself from fairy to vamp, from saint to slut. These were the words she used to explain her metamorphosis. "Today I am a vamp and a slut. Not a fairy and certainly not a saint!"

I had trouble imagining Natalia as a fairy because she was slightly taller than me, in fact she was in every way, both laterally and vertically, larger than me. Of course, it is possible that in another environment, in relation to someone else, she might consider herself a fairy. The notion of Natalia as a saint, meanwhile, was absurd. To my knowledge, saints are physically fragile, but their spirit is unbreakable. Their spirit is guided to a single, bright point, which is God, and God looks after their spirit, and that is why their thoughts don't stray along wayward paths. Natalia, however, was well nourished and energetic, but her poor spirit was lost. Heavenly virtue was something she expressed neither in thought nor deed, so the suggestion had to be bitter sarcasm.

And it was this that I found myself thinking when Veronica suddenly picked up the alarm clock on her stomach, placed it next to the wall and rolled onto her stomach. She raised her bottom, propped herself on her elbows and looked me right in the eye.

None of my clients had ever behaved like this before. Ever. It was wholly inappropriate. And this was just the beginning.

I looked at Veronica and didn't say a word, though obviously I should have put a stop to the situation there and then. In a gentle but firm voice, I should have said: "Natalia, please lie on your back. In this room we make progress through language, by speaking, by putting our emotions into words. So please, lie down."

But I didn't say a word.

Had curiosity suddenly put me in a headlock? Did I really want to know what it meant to be a "vamp" and a "slut" in these circumstances? Had the wig and strange clothes blurred my judgment, made me think I was watching a theater play? I have subsequently returned to this situation countless times. My initial hypothesis is that layer therapy involves the risk of the immersion fallacy, which in layman's terms might be described as the therapist's susceptibility to become deeply involved in the client's story. I believe this phenomenon—if, indeed, it exists—should be distinguished from countertransference (*Gegenübertragung*); after

all, immersion exists in organic symbiosis with the artistic potential of the client's exercises. It was these and other such premises
that I had thought of examining in my book, which I was already
eagerly developing in my free time.

Veronica clearly realized she was transgressing boundaries
because she said: "I can pay extra for this, if you want"—there
wasn't so much as a hint of an apologetic undertone in her voice,
and I got the distinct impression that she had no intention at all of
paying extra—"but, I hope you understand, this will really help
my healing process."

It would soon become clear just what *this* was. Veronica placed
her right hand between her legs, propped herself more firmly on
her left elbow and raised her bottom higher. Her skirt rose up and
I noticed that what I had initially thought were tights were in
fact stockings and suspenders, and she wasn't wearing any panties.
Her buttocks were ivory-white.

Veronica then began sliding a finger inside herself. She rubbed
the finger—I assumed—against both her labia and clitoris,
though of course I couldn't see any of this; all I saw was her face
and hand, sometimes disappearing further and deeper, and her
slowly gyrating bottom.

Veronica began to speak. Mumbling, slowly but without the
slightest hesitation, without fumbling for words, as though she
had practiced the entire routine in advance. Perhaps she had.

"In reality, this is just a brief moment that I will try to describe
in detail . . . This is what people generally call heterosexuality . . .
this is one example. I've heard people say all sorts of things about

sex, but believe it or not it's hard for me, I need this space, this paid moment, to muster the courage to talk about it . . . So let's begin."

Veronica paused briefly. She was collecting herself, moving slightly faster now, before latching onto something, or so I assumed, as she sighed loudly and let her bottom slump to the couch.

With this she continued the story and the movements.

"I am on top of him, he is inside me. The thing inside me, the thing that has temporarily commandeered his will, grows with our movements to its full size and fills me completely. His strong hands grip me, my backside, lift me, lower me, move me the way you move someone sitting on top of you, back and forth, up and down . . . I'd like to stop here for a moment. When I think about it, this movement confuses and dizzies me. You normally move things from one place to another, right? Objects are moved from A to B, it's perfectly ordinary, it's what people call 'doing' or maybe 'organizing,' 'sorting things out' . . . But this movement, the hands gripping my buttocks, lifting, lowering and moving me the way you move someone sitting on top of you, back and forth, up and down . . . At the end of the day, what's it all about?"

Veronica didn't wait for me to answer but continued without pause. "I once tried to start a conversation on this topic. I was with a friend, someone who back then I considered a bosom buddy, a kindred spirit who was always ready to share her wise advice about my relationship problems. Her partner was there too, a man I'd always thought was intelligent and trustworthy. We drank wine, we talked about intimate matters, and I plucked up the courage to ask what they thought about that very series of movements, that magical up-down-back-and-forth with which I was sure they were acquainted. My question was met with silence. They looked at each other in a way that made me instantly regret saying anything at all. My friend chuckled, which offended me a great deal, and her partner responded to her chuckle with a chuckle of his own—what profound mutual understanding must have existed between them . . . Then my friend turned to look at me and said, 'Darling, it's just shagging!' That's right, can you believe it? *It's just shagging!*"

This final word she spat out of her mouth in disgust, as though she despised "shagging," as though "shagging" were the worst thing she could ever imagine. Again, however, she didn't wait for my reaction but continued unfazed from the point where the conversation with her bosom buddy and her partner had dried up.

"In fact, this movement is something supernatural, indescribable. It's an energy that no human can harness for their own use . . . It's mindless in every respect, and it was such a waste . . . those strong hands that don't ask permission but move me back and forth, back and forth, back and forth . . ."

In retrospect, it was at this point that I should have interrupted her and put an end to proceedings, because she was talking nonsense and it irritated me. What did she mean that it was "a waste," that it was "mindless"? "An energy that no human can harness for their own use" . . . Where on earth had she learned things like this? This is precisely how conception happens; there's nothing mystical about it. The same can be said of intercourse not for the purpose of procreation, an activity that has been practiced since the dawn of time. I've never understood the train of thought that describes penetration in almost supernatural terms. Of course, it can be depicted with words other than "shagging," and her selection of this particular word from all the possible words used to describe the act is revealing in itself. My gut feeling is that it conveys, among other things, an attempt at a level of brutality, it's an exaggerated understatement, if you will allow such an oxymoron. I could have explained that similar movements can be found outside the realm of sexual intercourse, such as in the back-and-forth movement of a piston, though Veronica certainly knew this just as well as I did. Is there anything mystical about the movement of a piston, anything "mindless"?

Instead, I remained quiet and allowed her to continue.

"And eventually he ejaculates . . . the thing he has turned into, the thing that has become his temporary, liquid will, flows inside me with all its force . . . the strong hands yank my backside down one final time . . . And this is my core experience, at this very moment . . . being held and consummated . . . And I can't help how good it feels . . . His moment has become my moment . . . I feel more ashamed of it as I speak about it . . . And I don't understand where the shame comes from, whether it is shame at all . . . or something else altogether . . . The sensation rushes inside me with the same force as that final yank, the downward pull, and after that everything, everything is over . . . and still, despite the shame, despite the fact that I've stopped believing in love . . . I can still recall that sensation inside me . . . the feeling, the memory of being held and filled makes my vagina clench . . ."

After this, Veronica brought herself to climax right there in front of me. She squirmed, panted, and eventually allowed the full weight of her body to slump across her arms, moaning in the way women have learned to moan in these situations, as if she didn't feel one iota of shame.

And from that position, from somewhere deep within her slumped body, the breathless panting, the sticky sweatiness, Veronica propped herself up on her elbows and looked me right in the eye, and her face was empty, so expressionless that it almost frightened me.

"The saddest thing about all this is that when I talk about it now, when I tell you this, it's not lewd, not depraved, not even exciting, it's nothing that the two of us could share. It's just bland, boring, numbing and—and this is the most ludicrous thing of all—it's still real and precise. Please explain this to me, Doctor!"

She pulled the wig from her head, rolled onto her back and buried her face in her hands. She started to cry, and I am still unsure whether those tears were genuine or not. Was this her money shot, the climax she'd been building up to all along?

I handed Natalia a tissue, she snatched it and blew her nose. I glanced at the clock: there was plenty of time left. I had a thought. I looked at her and the enormous alarm clock that she had stuck in the gap between the couch and the wall, a gap that Veronica's back-and-forth movements had made larger still. I decided to take a risk and ask Veronica to visit us again. Veronica clearly moved in different circles than Natalia, who could only fumble around the unlit corridors of her memories and obsessions. Besides, Veronica's very name was, if not a key to Natalia's world, then at least a very good picklock: *vera icon*, "real image," a mirage more real than deceptive words. I sensed that Natalia was on the verge of a decisive catharsis.

RECOVERY PROGRAM
WEEK 9

Instruction: Invite Veronica to our session.
Use the present tense.
Key word: vermouth

As a therapist, I think of my clients' quirks and whims like surprise gifts; I gratefully accept them. In this regard, I follow Dąbrowski's thoughts on development potential, a theory that views personality disturbances as a positive thing, as the structural pillars of a creative personality. The therapy room is a safe space in which together we can sow, turn, layer and shape the material that comes to light. In this way we can construct a resilient mind, one that is not satisfied with knowing only itself (*gnothi sauton*), but one that also strives to take care of itself (*epimelēsthai sautou*).

Natalia agreed to my proposed exercise with particular gusto. This didn't surprise me. To turn her nose up at it would be to suggest that her masturbation performance wasn't such a big deal, nothing but throwing ideas around, which naturally could not be the case. And Natalia knew it. It was as though there was a small child having a tantrum inside her, a child who would take a pair of scissors to her mother's pearl necklace simply to see whether motherly love would cease at the moment the pearls tinkled across the floor. But it doesn't cease. We deal with it. We can see past the antics, we know that, deep down, such behavior is actually a show of trust. We offer our merciful calm like a punching bag that can be struck with full force.

Only once have I cut short a therapy program because of a client's behavior. It happened at the beginning of my career when I was still very inexperienced and didn't know how to deal with a pathological liar. A smart-looking young man appeared at my office and told me he had a fear of commitment. By our third meeting, flagrant contradictions began to appear in his stories—there was no other way to explain them. First the man's father was a former Stasi spy, then a pastor in Lapland. This was still within the bounds of possibility; men who live to a grand old age have time to change their guise many times over. However, it is categorically not possible for a mother to be simultaneously alive and dead. At first the man claimed that his mother had died in his final year of high school from an acute inflammation of the pancreas caused by excessive alcohol use, but at our next session his drunken mother reappeared to hand her son a bunch of flowers as he graduated from college. "She was my stepmother, but I called her my mother," the man explained with a straight face when I asked about it, apparently thinking I was so gullible that I would swallow three improbable statements hook, line and sinker: (1) that a former spy turned pastor would twice take an alcoholic as his wife, (2) that anyone would ever call their stepmother their mother, and (3) that this particular young man with his fear of commitment would call his erratic stepmother, a woman who caused him numerous disappointments, his own mother.

I sent him away. I wouldn't do such a thing nowadays, though I'm perfectly aware that pathological liars are beyond cure. With the experience I have now, I would have asked him to layer his stories. If he really wanted to survive in this world, at the very least he should learn to commit to his own lies.

I should probably have cut short Natalia's therapy program after the Veronica stunt, and certainly would have, had it not been for my PhD and my profound understanding of human emotions. At my age, I'm also acutely aware of how wholly unethical it would have been to end Natalia's treatment, particularly as I had allowed everything to happen in the first place. I alone must take responsibility for this, there are no two ways about it. Natalia trusted my judgment as a therapist. Abandoning her in this situation would have been a grave professional error.

As for the boundary between reality and fiction, it should be noted that the factual value of the exercises used in layer therapy is of little significance. The whole point is that the exercises allow the client to reveal their inner reality through art. Perhaps Natalia's hospital fantasy was a part of her imaginary sensory world. When she claimed in her letter to have been treated at a psychiatric ward, was she in fact begging me for the care she felt had previously been denied her? I had resolved to return to the subject at a suitable time, but for the moment I didn't want to jeopardize the therapy's progress. Natalia might consider my focus on her lies as an accusation and suddenly hit the brakes.

I quickly recovered from the shock that Natalia's masturbation (and my own unwitting voyeuristic role in it) had caused me. Now that we had embarked on this path, I realized we would have to continue along it until we reached the end. "The flawed corkscrew," as I described her masturbatory performance in my notes, was ultimately a perfectly logical step after her Saint Phalle revelations. In this respect Natalia took the primal scene into her own hands, *après coup*.

Don't worry, allow me to explain this claim! In psychoanalytical literature, the primal scene is called the *Urszene*, a term I personally try to avoid because I am sensitive to the associations that words can have. Unfortunately, the German term always makes me think of the poisonous stench of urea and arsenic, and this is why at international seminars I prefer to use the French term *scène primitive*, which is now as established a term as the original *Urszene*.

What exactly happened in this room last time? The answer is astonishingly simple. Using Veronica as an accessory, Natalia constructed her own primal scene right there on my couch. She staged a sexual partner for herself and performed the role of the lover, but the strong hands moving her up and down didn't belong to this lover. In this spiraling spectacle interlacing past and present, she finally dared to face the greatest sorrow of her childhood with her whole body, not merely her frontal lobe. Under my protective gaze she found the courage to turn into a swan ready to take flight, a mole burrowing into the earth. Buoyed on waves of desire, she became her own mother, and with the hand delving beneath her she became her father too. She was a mother-father conglomeration, their shared enjoyment without the aim of reproduction, the act from which she had been banished decades ago, condemned to an orbit of comfortless Melancholy.

This was the crux of the matter: the tightly sewn seams of Natalia's inner space were beginning to come apart, and now she needed a sharper pair of scissors.

So I decided to turn up the heat slightly. I encouraged Natalia to set her memories aside and focus her attention on the present moment. I suggested that in the next exercise she avail herself of the shameless Veronica, daughter of the Sybarites. I gave her a single key word, *vermouth*, which I knew was a risky choice, but it was a noun that opened up countless possibilities. The word not only refers to the bitter key to understanding, that is, an intoxicant distilled from wormwood; crucially, it also contains many hidden clues, bait that I hoped Natalia would take. In Spanish the verb *ver* denotes seeing and watching. Like the French *voir* and Italian *vedere*, *ver* derives from the Latin present-tense infinitive *vidēre*, which denotes seeing, watching and understanding, and which has in turn given us the word "video"—*videō* meaning "I see." I hardly have to explain what the latter half of the word invokes, let alone the German associations of courage (*Mut*) and motherhood (*Mutti*) that she might derive from its pronunciation.

I admit that my expectations were high when Natalia left my office with her instructions. And I can't say I was surprised when she called me the following Monday and canceled our Tuesday session, claiming she had come down with something she called "man flu" and was now bedridden. Her voice wasn't at all hoarse, but I played along because I realized she needed more time to prepare.

The following Monday, she called to cancel our Tuesday session for a second time. Apparently she had tried to get back on her feet too early and her temperature had gone up again. By now I was starting to worry about her but decided to channel my unrest into something useful and began planning the outline of my forthcoming book.

When Natalia finally arrived at my office after a three-week break, I barely recognized her. She had dyed her blond hair black and fashioned huge curls above her bangs. The neutral everyday makeup, which she had used to correct the slight asymmetry in her face, was gone. Her skin was powdered chalk-white, and around the cheekbones she had dabbed a peachy red, which against the unnatural white of the skin made her look almost like a clown. She had drawn thick pencil edges around her ever-vigilant eyes, and her eyelashes were so thick and black that they had to be fake. Her lipstick was the same shade of peachy red as her cheek, while the edging around the lips was in a darker hue, cherry-red. She was wearing a floral dress that widened at the hem and which she had tightened around the waist with a belt to make it more figure-hugging. The rigid, sharp frame of her bra made her breasts stand out prominently from the front of her dress.

"Hi," she said with a smile, swinging her hips as though to

make sure I realized how exceptional all this was. Then she handed me a tablet computer.

"Switch it on."

I opened up the fake-leather cover, folded it and propped the tablet on the table. The screen asked for a security code. "Veronica did as you told her," Natalia simpered. "Veronica has been for a little adventure! I'll tell you what happened once the video is running."

Natalia lay down on the couch, pulled her knees up, and placed the alarm clock between her legs, amid the folds of her dress. "Are you ready, Doctor?" she chirped. "The security pattern is a letter *Z* the wrong way round."

For a moment I wondered quite what she meant. Did she mean a mirror image of the letter *Z*, a letter *Z* on its side, in which case it was in fact an *N* or a mirror image of the letter *N*? I decided to try. I ran my fingers across the dots on the screen in a mirror image of the letter *Z*. My guess was right; a video appeared. I pressed the Play triangle.

One letter at a time, the text *THE DOUBLE LIFE OF VERONICA* appeared on the screen. The slow appearance of the letters was accompanied by music I didn't recognize. A woman was singing in a soft, purring voice about her toxic lover—and how it was a toxin she loved. "This is a French-Israeli artist by the name of Yaël Naïm," Natalia quickly explained. "The song was originally written for Britney Spears, but this version is far superior."

The film began. In the first scene, Veronica was standing in

front of a bathroom mirror. Filming everything was a cell phone
on a camera stand attached to a towel rack behind her. She was
applying dye to her hair with a large brush, humming a melody
just perceptible as the sighing of the song heard a moment ago.
"As you can hear, I'm constantly out of tune," Natalia laughed,
her laughter ensuring that, at least in this respect, I didn't think
she had too many expectations of herself. "As I told you back in
our first session, I don't have an ear for music."

Once Veronica had carefully spread the dye through her hair,
she covered her head in a protective plastic hat, looked via the
mirror into the camera, and winked.

In the next scene, Veronica was sitting at the kitchen table
and talking on the phone. The table was covered in oilcloth with
images of figs, bananas and Jerusalem artichokes. Veronica's voice
could barely be heard as the soundtrack for this scene was a disco
hit, its mood at once jaunty and oppressive. "This is Soft Cell's
'Darker Times,'" Natalia informed me. "It's my going-out song. I
always listen to this when I'm getting ready for a boozy night out."

In this scene, Veronica's makeup was even more lurid than
Natalia's. The dark, cat-like lines around her eyelids were very
thick and edged. They rose up steeply at an angle, joining her
well-defined eyebrows around the temples. Veronica had painted
her lips in a fiery red. Above her upper lip, on the left side of the
perioral area around the mouth, she had affixed a small, glittering
round jewel, which I assumed was a sticker because now, at least,
Natalia didn't appear to have any actual piercings in that area.

Veronica's black hair gleamed, almost blue. It seemed that the lights in the room had been adjusted specifically to achieve this effect. Veronica had blow-dried sections of her hair to form a shiny, silky wave covering her right eye, and she was constantly adjusting this *peekaboo* look with the forefinger of her free hand.

Veronica ended the call and placed the phone on the table. She raised her hand, spread her forefinger and middle finger into a *V* and showed it to the camera. She raised her chin a fraction, squinted her eyes. From beneath this attempt at come-hither eyes, she raised the corners of her mouth into a fake, lifeless smile, opening her lips just enough that her teeth showed, and in doing so raised the middle of her upper lip almost violently. With this expression, her face froze.

A few seconds passed until suddenly the image began flashing like strobe lighting in a kaleidoscope of bright colors: first egg-yolk yellow, then turquoise, then pink, then violet, blue, orange . . . "Andy Warhol," Natalia sighed from the couch, her voice oozing satisfaction.

The comment was almost moving. What trouble Natalia had gone to over this video! Now she lay there following it simply by the soundtrack (she couldn't see a thing), giving me a carefully timed voice-over so that not even the smallest detail would escape my attention.

The third scene transported us to the dance floor at a local dive. Veronica was holding her phone, the image was quivering and moving erratically. The camera switched between filming herds of people swaying and braying on the dance floor, and Veronica herself. A tall man with a ponytail was lurking around her; his pockmarked face came clearly into view every time he pressed his mouth against her neck.

Juice Leskinen's "Marilyn" was playing in the background, a song I instantly recognized. I laughed out loud as Veronica pulled the camera toward her mouth and whispered in time with the music, *I always feel best when I look at your chest*, so close that the camera lens steamed up.

The fourth scene consisted of still images and aggressive music that again I was unfamiliar with. In the first image was a full bottle of vermouth bianco and four empty shot glasses arranged around the bottle in a semicircle. In the next image, all the glasses were full. In the third image, the two glasses on the left were half full and the two on the right were empty. In the fourth image, the two middle glasses were half full and the two at the edge empty. Half full, empty, half full, empty. Empty, half full, empty, half full. An image in which the left-hand glass was full; in the next it was three-quarters full; in the next half full while the right-hand one was empty. An image in which the amount of liquid ranging from full, three-quarters full, half full and empty ran from right to left. In the final image the bottle of vermouth was empty, lying on its side.

"I guess you don't recognize this song," said Natalia. "It's 'Was ist ist' by Einstürzende Neubauten. But you'll recognize the next one, I'm sure of it."

The fifth scene began with music that I recognized from the very first bar. Sibelius's *Finlandia*, I assume in a concert performance as the soundtrack began with applause. At first the image onscreen was nothing but blue. The brass blared ominously and the timpani boomed as the blue silk scarf covering the camera was pulled aside.

A large bed came into view. Behind the headboard was the glimmer of a copper-colored curtain. Veronica was sitting on the left side of the bed, in profile to the camera, and in the same position behind her sat a dark-haired man I hadn't seen before. On the right side of the bed, again in profile, sat a red-haired woman, she too a new acquaintance. The static image was broken by the ponytailed man from the bar walking toward the bed with the blue silk scarf in his hand. He angled the pink CD player on the bedside table toward the bed and turned up the volume on *Finlandia*. Then he came to a stop in front of the red-haired woman, tied the scarf around her neck and pushed her backward onto the bed. All four of them were naked.

The ponytailed man placed two plump pillows beneath the red-haired woman's head and clambered on top of her. With his thighs he gripped the woman's upper body, pinning her arms against her sides, the way one might give a horse a signal to giddyup. Using her lips, the woman took the man's erect penis in her mouth and started sucking.

By now the dark-haired man was lying across the bed too. He lay down next to the redhead, behind the pillows, his face out of view. Veronica climbed on top of him and, in the traditional nomenclature for this position, she began to ride him.

The strings resonated, the percussion thundered. Veronica and the ponytailed man moved back and forth, each in their own space, sometimes slowly, sometimes faster, like mirror images. They craned toward each other, gripped each other's necks with opposite hands and pulled each other closer.

"This is the Mannerheim Suite of a famous hotel," Natalia explained. "The man with the ponytail is Rafael. We meet only rarely, because we both know we're bad company for each other. But sometimes even I need to stray from the straight and narrow, to release the pressure that's built up inside me. And so we help each other. As you can see right here in this video."

Natalia laughed. Veronica and Rafael began kissing.

"Rafael and I came up with a plan, it went like this: I would book a room for the night and bring a bottle of liqueur, no stronger than fortified wine so we didn't end up incapacitated. The key word you gave me—vermouth—suited this purpose excellently. We would go dancing at some low-grade dive, the kind of place where among all the pathetic drunkards we would meet young, open-minded people, the kind of people whose night is still young at two a.m. So we looked to this demographic to find ourselves some playmates."

There was something in Natalia's voice that told me this wasn't the first time she'd done this sort of thing. Perhaps these home videos were also an essential part of "straying from the straight and narrow," as she put it.

"I booked us a hotel room—this time a suite, because I wanted a handsome background for the film's final scene," she continued. "Our agreement specified that we would have sex within four clearly defined parameters: (1) Rafael would only penetrate the other woman, (2) the other man would only penetrate me, (3) Rafael would not kiss anyone but me, (4) I would not kiss anyone but him."

After a brief pause, Natalia cried out: "Doctor, do you see? This is the image of my sex life in its purest, most distilled form!"

While Natalia was narrating the scene, Rafael had shifted position. He had turned the red-haired woman onto her knees and was now banging her—I'm afraid there is simply no other verb to describe such monotonous shunting—from behind. Veronica had also moved and was now straddling the dark-haired man's face. From this cunnilingus position, she turned toward Rafael. They gripped each other by the arms and leaned diagonally closer to each other. The top of the red-haired woman's head was knocking against Veronica's side. As Rafael angled his head, Veronica's lips met his. Their upper bodies froze in this position, while they both began heaving their lower bodies against their respective partners with increasing vigor. Rafael moved back and forth inside the redhead, presumably in her vagina; he had slipped inside her with such ease that this surely couldn't be anal intercourse. Veronica ground her groin against the dark-haired man's mouth until she suddenly stopped, pulled away from Rafael's kiss and let out a moan that sounded almost like a yodel.

All of a sudden the screen went black.

Sibelius played on in the background.

Was there a fifth person in the room, someone who had placed a black cloth or piece of cardboard across the lens? If the music really was coming from the CD player in the room, as the ponytailed man suggested when he appeared to increase the volume, this sudden blackout just at the point of Veronica's climax confused me—unless there was a fifth person in the room.

Of course, it was possible that the CD player was merely a decoy and that *Finlandia* had been added to the recording afterward. If that was the case, someone would have had to increase the decibels of the soundtrack at precisely the moment the ponytailed man touched the volume knob on the CD player. It was possible, no doubt, but I was unsure as to whether a standard home video can have two independent sound files playing at the same time. Is it possible to combine the live sounds of the recording situation, which I assumed Veronica's eruption of pleasure must have been, with a recording of *Finlandia*, recorded in a different context and operating at differing volumes? Either Natalia or the person she had asked to do this for her had gone to a great deal of trouble to get the effect right.

In the final scene, Veronica was leaning against the marble tiles in the bathroom. Her makeup was washed off and the glittering jewel above her lip had disappeared. She looked tired, bedraggled, spent. The sound of running water. Perhaps they were preparing a bubble bath?

"There are no final credits," Veronica whispered to the camera. "But tell me, dearest doctor, did you find this even the *slightest* bit arousing?" She fell silent, then stared inquisitively at the camera for a moment before adding, "Is this something the two of us might share in some way?"

There was nothing to suggest that the subsequent conversation I had with Natalia about watching the film would be our last conversation regarding her treatment. I lowered the tablet to my lap and asked her a question, perhaps the most fundamental question possible after watching an exercise realized in this manner. "Have you wondered why it is that you need a witness—that is, me—for your sexual exploits?"

Natalia remained silent for a long time, but I was in no hurry. I could wait. "I don't know," she said eventually. "I'm sure you know. Do enlighten me."

It was only later, when I listened to the recording of our conversation, that I noticed how taut Natalia's voice sounded. It was abrupt, rude in a way I hadn't heard before. There was a hint of pent-up anger, something she tried to hide by articulating her words with almost exaggerated clarity.

At first I didn't pay this the slightest attention. I was in a euphoric state of mind. Once the film had finished, I was freed once and for all from the awkward feelings that Veronica's *entrée* three weeks earlier had caused me, and for which I use the term "immersion fallacy." What's more, that morning I'd received notice that the speech recognition program I had ordered from the United States, which could be plugged into the Olympus recorder, was waiting for me in the customs office. I had wanted to tell Natalia about this too.

Nowadays technical innovations are at a far more advanced level than when I was preparing my PhD, when word processing directly from speech seemed almost as much of a pipe dream as synthetic meat does now. I don't even want to think about the number of hours I spent laboriously typing out transcriptions. I saw clients all day every day, then spent my evenings painstakingly banging our taped conversations into written form. The mass of text grew and grew, files came into being, folders within folders, giving birth to countless subfolders where I saved these new files, each with its own name, names like maria.doc, maria_2.doc, maria_15.doc, maria_maybeinclude.doc, maria_FINAL.doc, and so on and so forth. One way or another I survived, but I won't be embarking on a project like that ever again. Life is simply too short.

But now I could sense my own strength. My thoughts regarding the new book had crystallized during Natalia's three-week break. I even had a name: *Broken by Love*. I was keen to hear Natalia's thoughts on the name, and after this I could present her with the initial list of contents. I believe it is a credible format, both informative and entertaining. Finding a publisher wouldn't be a problem. In its sheer simplicity, the concept of the book is genius: I would be the sole author, and the content would be provided by Natalia herself—protected, of course, with anonymity. We would have to establish some common rules for how to proceed at the earliest convenience, but as it turned out Natalia was to deny me this opportunity.

No matter how many times I go over events in my mind, I can't find a single explanation for what happened next. It seems I had profoundly offended Natalia by refusing to go along with her little game; I refused to answer the question Veronica posed me at the end of the film, and instead, I started trying to draw my own interpretation. With great fervor, I might add! I felt such joy at being able to analyze the film that I'd assumed Natalia too would be gripped with enthusiasm.

I began telling her that perhaps this behavior, something we might term "exhibitionism," didn't actually have anything to do with her experiences. Perhaps more pertinently, she wanted *me* to experience things, and through my experience she sought to purify her own story.

Natalia listened in silence.

I continued. I told her I certainly believed that her mind could split into multiple personalities in intimate situations. The final proof of this was the strict separation of kissing and penetration. When Natalia entered the realm of passion, she was no longer able to combine the full spectrum of being with one and the same person, be it one of her lovers or herself. She couldn't find a core within herself, not even a paltry replica of a core, somewhere she could have stored her emotions and senses the better to deal with them later. And so she compartmentalized her experiences, bagged them up and froze them as and when they presented themselves. She tore herself open like a fish ready for gutting and withdrew (in the figurative sense of the word) from the situation at hand.

Natalia did not argue with this.

"This is why you need therapy," I continued. "You need me specifically because I am not one of your lovers." With these direct words, I reminded her of the fundamental principle upon which all strands of therapy must be based.

Natalia remained silent.

"I am at your disposal for forty-five minutes each week at a cost of eighty-five euros," I reminded her. "That means our session costs 1.90 euros per minute and 0.03 euros per second." I use these numbers in training sessions too, when I explain to a room full of therapists and psychoanalysis students that a single second can change the course of a life. That's all the time it takes to experience a painful memory, a shocking revelation, intoxicating pleasure, death.

In this hall of mirrors that we call life, Natalia saw me as the only person free of reflections. And it was all because of money. And time. I needed her to realize this.

"Ultimately this is about time," I continued. "That's how layer therapy works. It offers the client condensed chunks of time, like diamonds shining a phosphorescent light into the darkness. I give you a stimulus, you write something down, and afterward we exchange our thoughts. Little by little, our conversations form a gleaming column of sunlight, a vertical bridge in whose glow experiences and the thoughts they elicit can be brought closer together, one gentle tug at a time. The end result is the sensory, sweet-tasting union of life and understanding. To put it one way, it is forgiveness. To put it another way, it is peace."

Natalia did not make a sound.

I continued.

"For our next session, I think we should put *Ear-Mouth* back in its proper place. Are you ready to see it again? I really sense that the time is right."

The words flowed from my mouth of their own accord. I didn't have to guide them, coax or berate them, I simply allowed them to come, and they came and came and came.

"Do you know what this wonderful painting is fundamentally about? The name *Bouchoreille* refers to a short text by Paul Valéry, a text in which every word is sheer genius. Valéry writes: 'Puisque JE ME parle, c'est donc que JE sait ce que ME ne sait.' I have translated the words thus: 'If *I* speak to my*self*, I therefore know something my*self* does not.' The message of Elise Watteauville's painting is clear and unequivocal. A person's internal speech can easily remain trapped in the area of the 'ear-mouth,' the closed inner space of the psyche. Valéry believed, as do I and as Elise might have too, that there exists a way out of this circle: writing, the intercession of the hand, the act of making the voice flesh, as it were, making it visible. I have framed Valéry's observation and displayed it on my wall at home. And I wrote a PhD about it. This assertion lies at the heart of layer therapy, and nobody can take it away from me. This is why I love *Ear-Mouth*."

I took a deep breath and posed my final question to Natalia, though in my heart of hearts I already knew the answer. "Is that why you loved *Ear-Mouth* too?"

Natalia sat up on the couch.

"I feel unwell," she said, and she really did look a little queasy. "I don't want to vomit in your toilet, dear doctor. I want to go home. I'm leaving now."

She threw the alarm clock into her bag, tightened the straps of her floral dress and stood up. She held her right hand behind her back, making it plain that today we would not shake hands.

"I'll bring you the vulva next time," she said, now with that familiar cockiness in her voice that she used to try to rise above me. "I've already drawn the outlines; I'll have it finished in no time. See you next Tuesday. Bye!"

Natalia kept this promise. She arrived at my office a week later, alas for the last time. With her she brought the drawing and a text written in dialogue format, a text that didn't allow me to get a word in.

RECOVERY PROGRAM
WEEK 10

Instruction: Draw your vulva and let it speak.

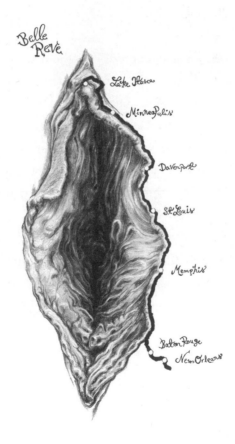

Well, my dearest doctor, here we are—finally! The *vittu* or *fittan*, *fyttan* or *votze*, *Fotze* or *futh*. To begin, allow me to take you back in time through Finnish, Swedish, Old Norse, Middle High German, Proto-High Germanic, Scots dialects and Old Icelandic all the way back to the Indo-European tongue from which it all began with the root word *pū*, meaning to "rot," "decompose," "go off," "stink," "stench."

Here we are.

I warn you, Doctor: today my thoughts stink. My body of words is as unwashed as Anushka in my stories . . .

Before we allow my vulva to take the floor, I would like to confess my sins. I know I have broken your rules. *Mea culpa!* I didn't come to our sessions when I should have. I have laid bare the details of my sexual proclivities in ways that perhaps you found offensive. I hope that one day you can find it in yourself to forgive me. I hope you also understand that a dog will always walk as far as its leash will allow.

I'd like to add that I will always be grateful to you. Working with you has calmed my restlessness. I no longer feel the constant compulsion to copulate, *ta-daa!* That's entirely thanks to you, my dear doctor, no one else.

Well, I believe my vulva wishes to interrupt me.

Am I speaking unclearly?

My mistress's perspective in this matter is very limited. Besides, she can only speak for herself. But because, exceptionally, I am today's guest of honor and because I have been encouraged to express my opinions freely, allow me to say the following.

From the outset, I hoped and wished that you would step up from your armchair and sit down near me. That I could have you inside me. There in the tight darkness, I oozed with expectant sap, because I could do nothing else. All I can do is flow.

The problem is that my mistress's confessions make me moist through and through. Just the joy of listening to her makes me twitch. Something happens here in this stylishly furnished room, something I guess doesn't happen when my mistress is cavorting in the bedroom with goodness-knows-whom. That feels good too, but it doesn't feel like this.

Once, when my mistress was crying over Ear-Mouth, you bravely came and sat down near me. You are such a good person, ready to bend the rules at the mere sight of tears. You comforted her, and you did the right thing; my mistress needed a paper tissue, not penetration.

But there were other moments too . . . countless other moments. I lie on the couch at my most open, slippery as an oyster. Weeping, sweating, oozing, and I cannot stop until the throbbing subsides.

If you can't help me in this regard, Doctor, you would be advised to wash the couch's orange upholstery and send me on my way because I am bad, bad, bad . . .

As you can see, I've drawn my genitals from a *dal sotto in sù* perspective. I knelt down, placed my phone on the floor between my legs, took a number of photos. Using my fingers, I held together my inner labia, my *nymphae*, closing them up and opening them again, pressing them gently together, pushing them first to the left, then to the right, then straightening them again, held between my forefinger and middle finger I pinched them in a straight line before finally prizing them wide open again.

In looking for the perfect image, I made a number of fascinating observations. Such as the fact that you really can shape the inner labia. They are not exactly playdough, but neither do they bounce straight back to their original position because there's no such thing. They don't have a fixed position. The labia remain for a moment in precisely the position in which I place them, before straightening out as they please. In Latin they are called the *labia minora*, though they're not really all that small. They're like Dumbo's ears, sometimes like the crinkled, dewlap folds around the edge of a chanterelle mushroom. And they are unique to every woman.

I wanted to see all their possible formations. I took fifteen different shots. Each image was different, and I realized that the potential for metamorphosis is endless.

I know you're skeptical of contemporary poetry, but even there one can find words of wisdom. In a recent volume, a certain renowned poet wrote the lines "the *vittu* is a drafty hallway" and "the vulva is a violet living room." It's a wonderful poem; its name is "The Names." That's exactly how I think of it: the *vittu* is for breeding, the vulva is for pleasure. The *vittu* is for passing through, the vulva is for taking one's time.

You once told me that language has all the power. And you were right. We don't talk about the "external reproductive organs" unless we are reproducing, right? And what kind of "external reproductive organ" is the clitoris anyway? Its sole purpose is to give women pleasure. We shouldn't speak of the "genital area" unless the intention is to have a funeral for the *Fotze*, because the very word is derived from the Latin *genitus*, which is the perfect participle of the verb *gignere*, which denotes one who has begotten, procreated, one who has already done all they can, given their all. Only the eulogy is missing—and this isn't one of them!

So, in carrying out this exercise, I spent a lot of time touching my inner labia, something I do very rarely unless I'm in a state of keen excitement. Well, and whenever I trim my pubic hair—I do shave down there, you know— though another famous poet once wrote a particularly critical poem on this subject. I'll never forget the first verse:

I never prune my forest. It is fragrant, buzzing.
On the crest of my flowing curls
your cock rides inside, cheering with joy.

Be that as it may, touching myself to shave is different from trying to construct an image from which to draw myself. Shaving is a far more practical affair, moving the lips and folds to one side, carefully making sure the blade doesn't cut the wrong places.

When I picked up the pencil, I felt something altogether different.

I couldn't decide which shot to use as the basis of my drawing. I flicked back and forth through the series of fifteen shots, looked at each image countless times. I slept on it, then continued flicking through and scrutinizing each of them in turn. After a while I couldn't see my genitals as part of the rest of my body anymore. The surrounding corporeality disappeared, and Georgia O'Keeffe's lewd flowers began to shine through. Do you realize what it was I was seeing? The extraordinary beauty of my *nymphae* revealed itself to me around the cleft of the vagina like a Japanese rose, one petal at a time. Visually speaking, the opening of the vagina is a boring place. Despite its moistness, it is sterile, anonymous, like any bodily orifice photographed with an endoscope—the mouth, the gut, the anus. But look at the clitoris! It stands proud like the stylized, art deco pistils of an arum lily, only in red. And look at the *labia minora*. Here we can see some of the plant kingdom's noblest specimens, poppy, hibiscus, pink pudica . . .

In the end I chose an image at random.

Then I drew a map.

My name is Belle Reve. As one who speaks French, you'll notice that everything is wrong with this name, and as a lover of art, you'll

*understand why. I've outstayed my welcome, as the saying goes, so
I'd better continue.*

Through me flows the great Mississippi, which as a child my
mistress used to call the Pissymissy. I became instantly attached to
the place, after all, the river delta is shaped almost like me, and I
liked the nickname because, after all, my principle function is to pass
urine. I think this is the best way to draw up a travel plan, to see a
new form above another old one, to see Italy as a boot, for instance,
Croatia as a pterosaur, Finland as a maiden, Argentina as a hitch-
hiking beaver, China as a flying witch, a river as a vulva, an island
as a heart. In this way, a place becomes your own.

The glades around my Mississippi don't have time to decompose
or rot, let alone to stink, because the current is so strong. My Mississippi sucks into its vortex whatever it wants. It's a perky Dixieland
band. It's a honky-tonk bar, where you just have to shout. (Don't
ask whether it's a saloon or a brothel, a casino or something else,
it's always something else.) It's "Für Elise" in ragtime, with all
those sassy, syncopated rhythms that big important doctors used to be
almost as worried about as they were about the debauching effects of
train travel on young women. It's a Greyhound with wings grown
fast to its tin sides. It's American Airlines, its landing gear pound-
ing curses from the runway. It's a kayak, of course it's a kayak. It is
water, sludge, being lost, being found, it is a mangrove tree stretching
its roots into the brown water.

My mistress claims she doesn't have an ear for music. It doesn't
matter one way or the other, because my Mississippi's melodies are
very simple. All you need is a set of drums, a bass and a whistle. Can

you whistle, Doctor? The boys in New Orleans sure can! There's a guy who slaps his fat bass in time with the drums while whistling a tune that really gets my Mississippi moving.

Two men, two instruments, two pairs of hands, one pair of lips. A dream orchestra playing my favorite tune at my behest: The Bobcats with—the one and only—Big Noise from Winnetka!

I first discovered the Mississippi in the early 1980s, looking through a world atlas when I was at home convalescing. The name filled me with glee, because I had just learned a painful new word from my mother, a word that to me meant stinging, burning and stomach cramps, a word that brought my temperature up, forcing me to see a doctor. The doctor wanted me to pee into a cup, but nothing came out. Apparently I had a bashful bladder. That was what my father called it, but my mother used a different word, and I ended up undergoing a procedure called suprapubic puncture, the third mystery surrounding my nether regions, the significance of which became apparent to me at far too young an age. But it was the doctor who talked about the suprapubic puncture, not my mother.

My mother had dressed me in a velvet, turquoise dress that was far too fancy for a trip to the doctor. But this turquoise dress was the only clean, appropriate one I had left, because before I fell ill I'd soiled all my summer skirts, and I needed to wear a skirt or a dress because I was piss-shy. This was the word I learned from my mother. I also learned that people who are piss-shy mustn't wear pants, at least they certainly mustn't wear jeans, because a defective downstairs doesn't like seams.

It was the word "piss-shy" that brought me to the banks of the Mississippi as I lay at home, a miserable little patient, flicking through an atlas I'd found on the bookshelf. I needed something to stimulate me, as my temperature had gone down and the pain had almost disappeared. It was a minor miracle, to be perfectly candid, because the pink antibiotic gel my mother squirted into my mouth was nothing but a placebo. The thick, foul-tasting gunk was made specially for children and even allegedly took children's tastes into account—what a foul lie that was! The substance was nauseatingly sweet and didn't taste remotely of the strawberries it claimed to simulate; it was more like glue laced with something acrid and saccharine. When I made her try the medicine herself, my mother conceded it tasted terrible. But still every day she forced it into my mouth in the syringe that had come with the package and wouldn't call the doctor and ask to have the medicine in tablet form, though I made it clear to everyone at the top of my lungs that I could swallow pills just like any adult.

There I lay on the sofa, flicking through maps, when suddenly a double page opened up showing the whole of North America, the place where in 1921 my grandmother's cousin had headed in a boat so that now once a year we received a *Meerrrryyyy Chriiiistmaaas* card with a picture of a chubby Santa Claus holding his stomach and ho-ho-hoing. I began examining this vast continent and quickly located the state of Michigan, where the Christmas cards came from. I found a little dot named Battle Creek, where my grandmother's cousin lived, and with that I allowed my eyes to roam the page.

That's when my eyes fell upon the Mississippi.

Can such a word really exist? The word hissed the way healthy pee hisses, and I started hissing it like a spell so that I might become healthy once and for all. As I hissed it, my lips turned the Mississippi into Pissymissy, and I divided the word in two. I understood what the first half meant.

"What does *missy* mean?" I asked my mother.

My mother told me that being *missy* meant being churlish and bad-tempered, and that in Mississippi no less, it was how people pronounced *messy*. My glee grew even more: exactly, that was me! Poor, miserable, stroppy little me, fed up that peeing had become so messy and painful.

And so I was baptized in my very own Mississippi, and it renamed me Pissymissy. There was a place for me in this world after all, an entire state, a river flowing from Lake Itasca, and I swore that one day I would dive into its balmy waters. Could things hold any more significance than this?

As my mistress seems to want to move backward in time instead of forward, as I would prefer, and as she deems it necessary to talk about urine instead of pleasure, which I would much rather we talk about, then so be it, let us spend another few moments staring in the rearview mirror. Do tell us another scatological story while you're on a roll, oh mistress mine. The clock's ticking! Tell us about the banknote on the bathroom door. Tell us about the time your father became exhilarated. There's plenty of time.

This isn't a pretty memory.

My father had the longest fuse in the world, except when he lost his temper. And when he lost his temper, he became really exhilarated. That was the word he used, and my mother and I used it too. I don't know who first came up with the word, but I know that there was nobody in this world who could become exhilarated quite like my father.

When the exhilaration started, my father's meek and mild expression disappeared. The world went black. Without exception, this happened only when I was disobedient. Not just a little bit naughty, but stratospherically naughty.

On this particular occasion, I'd taken the kitchen scissors from their hook.

I walked with the scissors in my hand. Snip-snap.

I was an ancient monster, hungry as a wolf. My nose was unbeatable, I could smell my prey from a distance. It was lounging on our green velvet sofa and didn't notice my arrival.

I took it completely off guard.

I think I should point out, dear doctor, that my mistress had various privileges not enjoyed by her friend next door, the girl constantly on the receiving end of her father's leather belt. In this respect, my mistress's physical integrity was preserved until the very end. Without fear of punishment, she could clown around, play to the gallery, even misbehave a little, she could caper here and there, nourish her imagination, just as long as she didn't play with me, because her parents believed that play was a child's most important function. In a word, my mistress's position was privileged. But not even her saintly parents could tolerate pure evil.

I attacked the cushion my grandmother had embroidered, though my original intention wasn't to harm it. All I meant to do was jump on its neck and shout *yee-haw*, because while I was walking around I'd stopped being an ancient monster and, snip-snap, I turned into a bison hunter, and so I ran toward the sofa, the scissors in my hand.

This was my first, if rather minor, transgression. This isn't what made my father exhilarated.

I leapt onto the sofa knees first, just as I had planned, shouted *yee-haw*, as I had planned, and raised the scissors into the air, victorious. I crawled on top of the cushion like a hunter who jumps from a horse's back and lands right on the bison's neck, changing into a fearless bison rider in the blink of an eye. I held the scissors above my head like a spear, ready to strike, and at that very moment my mother came into the room.

"Careful with those scissors!" she shouted.

"What on earth are you doing?" she continued shouting.

"I'm killing the bison!" I shouted back.

It was this sentence that caused my father such exhilaration.

If I had said, *I've killed the bison*, nothing would have happened. The game would have been over and done with and my imagination nourished once again. I could have handed my mother the scissors and given her a conciliatory smile.

But I told her I was on the bison's neck in the here and now, still in the process of killing it. I was gripping the cushion between my knees, I could smell the blood, the musk, I saw the panic in the whites of the beast's eyes, the steam puffing from its nostrils, I saw the flesh, the guts, heard it groan as it took its final breath.

In a flash I started stabbing the scissors into the cushion.

I struck once, and when my mother shouted, I struck again. I struck the animal and looked up at her, struck and watched my mother's expression change from surprise to disbelief, from disbelief to anger, from anger to terror.

Then, out of nowhere, my mother was bellowing.

"Young lady, this stops right now!" she shouted.

But it didn't stop.

I struck new holes into the cushion, more rapidly now, my strokes no longer grandiose and curved, the length of a spear, but shallow, at close range, as though I were brandishing a small dagger, one after the other, I used the scissors to rip gashes in the cushion's upholstery. Beneath my grandmother's beautiful embroidery appeared another cushion, a run-of-the-mill light green thing, and I tore into its fabric too, and beneath the slashes there appeared clumps of white cotton wool.

I smelled the blood, the death, the heat, and my own impending end.

You really knew how to be a little rascal. And this wasn't the only time, was it? One summer Saturday you snatched the trowel your mother was using to till the carrot beds from right under her nose. She saw you coming and put the tool down. You were looking for a sweet, earthy snack, but your mother said, "Let them grow a bit more first." You grabbed the trowel and ran off. You ran for kilometers and hid it far away in the woods. The horror of this act sent you off-kilter. You could never remember where you'd hidden it.

At that point my father entered the room. He wasn't exactly walking but wasn't running either. He arrived the way a tanker arrives in a harbor, the way a train pulls up at the terminal, the way someone walks when they have reached their destination. He stood beside my mother, towering, and looked at me in silence.

I squealed and threw the scissors onto the coffee table.

I stared at them as though they were a poisonous snake.

I'm sorry, I'm sorry, I shouted, *mea maxima culpa*, but nobody heard me.

My father froze and steeled himself. First his face gri-
maced, then his body turned to stone. Eventually he opened
his mouth. He drew a deep breath and let out the next words
slowly, heavily, each syllable louder, more emphatic than
the last, more crackling and foreboding, more elevated and
crushing, until the final syllable fell, destroying the planet
as we knew it.

"JE-SUS CHRIST!"

Then his fist came thundering down on the coffee table.

*You crawled over the arm of the sofa and scuttled away. You ran into
the bathroom and locked the door. Your father followed behind you.
By now his feet were those of a giant, his fist was like an anvil as he
hammered the door. "Open up!" he hollered. But you didn't open
the door. You sat on top of me, there in a puddle of pee on the tiled
floor, and howled with fear.*

I heard my mother's quick, frantic steps, heard her faint
voice. "Don't break the door, darling, please." But my
exhilarated father wanted to destroy the door. After all, I
had destroyed the cushion.

*But tell us about the money! Tell us, who on earth tapes a 500-mark
note the size of a broadsheet to the bathroom door? That little detail
is perfect for this story. Besides, what story wouldn't benefit from a
little detail about money? Charles Dickens and Honoré de Balzac
knew this only too well, and the good doctor knows it too, the doctor*

who has so far earned 765 euros from treating you. By the end of the session that will be 85 euros more, if we can just get to the end of this story. And the story will end, eventually it too will come to an end, it'll end before the clock chimes . . .

In the region where I grew up, people were fiercely proud of the fact that our bald president, whose bust graced the 500-mark bill, went to school right in the heart of our county, in the same town where as a teenager I moved to live with my grandmother. The new bill was presented in the centerfold of our local newspaper in September 1975, when it was introduced in honor of the president's seventy-fifth birthday. My parents had married that summer, they were head over heels in love. They did *it*, they did what was expected of them, that is, they made me, and after this by all rights they should have stopped doing *it*; after all, I'd already been born.

Nonetheless, in the year of my conception they removed this centerfold from the newspaper and attached it to the inside of the bathroom door with tape.

I never asked my parents why they had decided to display the banknote. And why on earth had they chosen to attach President Kekkonen, of all people, to the bathroom door to watch over us while we went about our business. Did they admire him and his party so greatly? Or was it the opposite sentiment? Did they hanker after riches and prosperity? Or was putting Kekkonen's image on the bathroom door their way of saying "Let the lions keep their candy"? Were they leftists? Were they conservatives? On the other hand, they were so profoundly apolitical, at least after I was born, that displaying a poster of a banknote on the bathroom door must have been some kind of ironic humor. Whenever they needed the bathroom, they talked about "going to pay their respects."

It's also possible that as they sat there pooing, they stared right past President Kekkonen, that in that blissful moment of anal meditation they stared instead at the wintry lakeside landscape that opened up behind him, the most famous panorama in our county.

As a child, it didn't matter to me why the banknote was stuck to the bathroom door. At that age I never wondered why my grandmother had nailed a gruesome crucifix to the wall behind her bed, or why during Holy Week she attached to it an even more gruesome plastic effigy of Christ. So I learned to urinate and defecate into the toilet like a big girl under the thick-rimmed, bespectacled gaze of Urho Kaleva Kekkonen, and that was that.

Behind that door, on the day of my father's exhilaration, I cowered flat on the floor in my own wee and howled until I suddenly stopped howling, because I'd had a miraculous idea.

Your father didn't usually get involved with issues of child-rearing, electing instead to let the women deal with women's matters by them-

selves. It was enough for him to serve as an example. The women scuttled here and there, nodding and nagging, eternally repeating their nagging, spinning a wheel of prohibitions and concessions until gradually the child became like thread, a dense, fleeced, tangled fiber, a yarn spun from the loom, something tangible, a cardigan, a cotton glove. But sometimes, when you went too far, your exemplary father lost his temper and informed you, in his characteristic way, exactly where the boundaries were. He fetched a tool kit from the lower shelf in the closet, took out a screwdriver, unscrewed the lock on the bathroom door, and saw your lifeless body on the floor. Your death did not move him. Your mother cried until her eyes were dry, lifted you up and carried you to bed, where you continued your little game throughout the following day. It's no wonder she was unable to bring you up like a proper child. You weren't a child. You were a nightmare. You were unbridled. You were you.

NATALIA'S BOOKSHELF

SIMONE DE BEAUVOIR: *She Came to Stay*. Translated by Yvonne Moyse and Roger Senhouse. London: HarperCollins, 1975. Originally published as *L'invitée* (Paris: Éditions Gallimard, 1943).

JUDITH BUTLER: *Gender Trouble: Feminism and the Subversion of Identity*. New York: Routledge, 1990.

HÉLÈNE CIXOUS: *"Coming to Writing" and Other Essays*. Edited by Deborah Jenson. Translated by Deborah Jenson, Sarah Connell, Ann Liddle, and Susan Sellars. Cambridge, MA: Harvard University Press, 1999.

JACQUES DERRIDA: *Of Grammatology*. Translated by Gayatri Chakravorty Spivak. Baltimore, MD: Johns Hopkins University Press, 2016. Originally published as *De la grammatologie* (Paris: Les Éditions de Minuit, 1967).

EVE ENSLER: *The Vagina Monologues*. New York: Dramatists Play Service, 1998.

MICHEL FOUCAULT: *The History of Sexuality I–III*. Translated by

Robert Hurley. New York: Vintage, 1990. Originally published as *Histoire de la sexualité I–III* (Paris: Éditions Gallimard, 1976–1984).

MICHEL FOUCAULT: "Technologies of the Self." In *Technologies of the Self: A Seminar with Michel Foucault*, ed. Luther H. Martin, Huck Gutman, and Patrick H. Hutton, 16–49. Amherst: University of Massachusetts Press, 1988.

NAOKO HAYASHI: "La voix dans le dialogue avec soi-même chez Paul Valéry" [The voice in dialogue with itself in the works of Paul Valéry]. *Gallia* 35 (1995): 43–50.

MARKUS O. KAARTINEN: *Donkey Milk*. Helsinki: Otava, 1983.

UUNO KAILAS: "Helvetti" [Hell]. The quotation on page 99 is from this poem, written in the late 1920s and first published on the back cover of *Nuori Voima*, May 1996.

RIINA KATAJAVUORI: *Maailma tuulenkaatama* [The world collapsed by the wind]. Helsinki: Tammi, 2018. The quotation on page 208 is from the poem "Nimet" [The names].

EEVA KILPI: *Tamara*. Helsinki: WSOY, 1972.

FREYJA KULKUNEN: *Latter Summer Gods*. Helsinki: Poesia, 2017. The quotation on page 209 is from page 33 in Kulkunen's book.

VEIJO MERI: *Sanojen synty* [The birth of words]. Helsinki: Gummerus, 1982.

ELINA REENKOLA: *Intohimoinen nainen: Psykoanalyyttisia tutkielmia halusta, rakkaudesta ja häpeästä* [A woman of passion: Psychoanalytical studies of desire, love and shame]. Helsinki: Gaudeamus, 2006.

PHILIP ROTH: *Portnoy's Complaint*. New York: Random House, 1969.

NATHALIE SARRAUTE: *Childhood*. Translated by Barbara Wright. Chicago: University of Chicago Press, 2013. Originally published as *Enfance* (Paris: Éditions Gallimard, 1983).

NATHALIE SARRAUTE: *Martereau*. Translated by Maria Jolas. Champaign, IL: Dalkey Archive Press, 2004. Originally published as *Martereau* (Paris: Éditions Gallimard, 1953).

SOPHOCLES: *Electra*. Edited and translated by David Raeburn. New York: Penguin Classics, 2008.

LIV STRÖMQUIST: *Fruit of Knowledge*. Translated by Melissa Bowers. London: Virago Press, 2018. Originally published as *Kunskapens frukt* (Stockholm: Ordfront/Galago, 2014). The quotation on page 28 is from page 36 of Strömquist's book, where she quotes Jean-Paul Sartre's *L'être et le néant* (Paris: Éditions Gallimard, 1943).

TUOMAS TIMONEN: *Oodi rakkaudelle* [Ode to love]. Helsinki: Teos, 2007.

JOUKO TURKKA: *Aiheita* [Subjects]. Helsinki: Otava, 1982. The quotation on page 139 is from page 24 of this book.

PAUL VALÉRY: "Langage" [Language]. In *Cahiers I*, ed. Judith Robinson. Paris: Éditions Gallimard / Bibliothèque de la Pléiade, 1973.

TENNESSEE WILLIAMS: *A Streetcar Named Desire*. New York: New Directions Publishing, 1980 (1947).